Crisis

The roots are the last to dry

Jorge Majfud

ILLEGAL HUMANUS
San Diego-Acapulco

Crisis
© Jorge Majfud
2012, Baile del Sol, Spain.
2019, 2020, 2021, Rebelde Ed.
© *Crisis. The roots are the last to dry*
© *Illegal Humanus, USA*
ISBN: 978-1-956760-25-5
Cover illustration:
"Christies World" by Ernesto Camacho, NY.
Av. Cuauhtémoc II. Acapulco, Mexico.
Email: cuauhtemoceditorial@gmail.com

SAN SEBASTIÁN NOPALERA, A SMALL TOWN *in the Sierra of Oaxaca, Mexico, has five thousand registered inhabitants, but only half of them live there. The lands that once produced coffee now barely yield corn, and there are almost no hands to harvest more. Its inhabitants, mostly women and children, survive on the aid sent by their men working in the plantations of the United States.*

Like in a war between two countries, every year a hundred or two hundred migrants return to Oaxaca in coffins. The jobs they are destined for are almost as deadly as crossing the border.

But not all who stay are women, nor are all who leave men. Like her brother, one day María Isabel Vásquez Jiménez decided to go to the other side with the promise of helping her widowed mother and returning in three years with enough capital to start a small business.

On February 11, 2009, the 17-year-old girl left her village and contacted a coyote in Putla de Guerrero who helped her cross the border. Three months later, on May 11, she found work at a vineyard of the West Coast Grape Farming Company, *near Modesto, California.*

Like María, the Mexican indigenous people who barely speak Spanish in California are the Hispanics who dedicate themselves to the pizca, *to pizcar, words that, like so many others in Spanglish, were created from the material of English—* pick up, *to pick—and shaped by the conjugation of Spanish.*

Perhaps we can never imagine María's fears when leaving her village at such a young age and with so little knowledge of the outside world, her nerves when arriving in Putla to contact a coyote, the vertigo and exhaustion of her journey through illegality. Perhaps she was happy on one of the three days she worked in the pizca. Almost certainly, she must have been happy resting beside her boyfriend, Florentino Bautista, another undocumented immigrant with whom she lived and planned to marry before returning to Mexico in three years.

But something went wrong. On May 14, the thermometer showed almost forty degrees Celsius in the shade. After nine hours under the sun, pruning vine shoots, María felt dizzy. Staggering, she walked toward her boyfriend and collapsed before reaching him.

Florentino asked for help and tried to revive her. The supervisor told him not to worry. Those fainting spells were normal.

—Put some alcohol on her, and she'll be fine—, he said.

But María remained unconscious.

They placed her in the truck that took the crew to their homes and waited for the departure time.

The cold water compresses and alcohol rubs had no effect, and the truck driver decided to take her to a doctor. María was burning with fever in the frightened arms of her companion. On the way, Florentino received a call from the vineyard supervisor, Raúl Martínez, reminding him that his girlfriend was a minor, so in his statement, he should say that she had fainted while exercising to stay in shape.

They arrived at the clinic at 5:15. When the doctors realized that María had a temperature higher than a human can withstand, they urgently transferred her to Lodi Memorial Hospital.

Two days later, María and her two-month-old fetus died of heatstroke. The medical report mentions heart failure.

Her boyfriend, Florentino, has not returned to work. He has also not received any calls on his cell phone. But the district attorney, James Willett, has charged María De Los Ángeles

Colunga, the owner of the labor company, Elías Armenta, the security director, and supervisor Raúl Martínez for failing to provide workers with shade and water, for lacking assistance in case of heatstroke, and for lying during the process.

The Mexican government, as is its custom, expressed its concern over the unjust conditions in which Mexicans work in the United States.

For his part, the governor of California, Arnold Schwarzenegger, also lamented María's death, though there was no mention of her unborn child. Years earlier, as governor, Schwarzenegger had promoted laws aimed at preventing such deaths from heatstroke.

Like María, Schwarzenegger was once an illegal immigrant in his youth, though his effort and sweat were spent in a Santa Monica gym, not in agricultural fields. Today, he is better known worldwide as the actor who in 1984 brought to life the cyborg Terminator. The film is not without its hidden paradoxes. The Terminator, the man-machine sent by intelligent machines from 2029 to the year 1984, had the objective of ending human resistance by eliminating the future rebel leader— not to say guerrilla fighter—before he was born. In its Hollywood remake of Herod, the nearly invincible machine is defeated by the human couple, and the mother of the future rebel,

Sarah Connor, manages to escape. In an open ending, Sarah—Sarai—appears months later in Mexico. At a gas station—the quintessential space of the American spirit—a Mexican boy takes her photograph, which will travel through time into the hands of her son and then her father. From this mythical story, one could infer that John, the rebel leader, could have been a Mexican or a citizen of any other Latin American country, perhaps the son of an illegal immigrant fleeing her own land.

John, or Juan, would be twenty-five years old today and would likely be crossing the border, more or less around this time, illegally. But if his mother had been Mexican, like María, he might have had to face a nightmare worse than that of the cyborg Terminator *and the future rebel might never have been born due to the successful enterprise of an inhumane group.*

On Wednesday, May 27, 2009, María's body left St. Anne's Catholic Church in Lodi, California. On Friday the 29th, it passed through Asunción Nochixtlán in a white coffin and, after six hours of travel, arrived in her village in the mountains. Her humble bedroom became the funeral chapel. At the head of the room, they placed the photo of her smiling, taken shortly before her departure. Below it, a wreath of flowers and a new debt for her mother.

María and her unborn child were buried dressed as a bride, as a mother bride. There was no Mass, because the village had no priest, and none could make it to the village chapel.

In María's empty bedroom, Jovita Margarita Jiménez Bautista remained, gazing at the smiling photograph of her daughter. Her widowed mother, or whatever she is called. Because in Spanish, there are names for a child who loses a mother, for a mother who loses her husband, but there is no name for a mother who loses a daughter. Surely, in no language is there a name for so much pain and so much injustice.

Friday, May 2. Dow Jones: 13,058
Sierra Vista, Arizona. 11:10 PM

On a moonless night, Guadalupe de Blanco crossed the border on her knees. She ate the desert sand and watered the soil of Arizona with the blood from her feet.

On Saturday the 3rd, in the afternoon, she stumbled upon a warm water bottle, one of those that the brother dogs leave in the desert in hopes of saving some dying soul.

On Sunday, she fell asleep very slowly, hoping not to wake up the next day. But she did wake up, nearly suffocated on a large stain her body had left on the stone. She recognized the vaginal halo of the Guadalupe who had cradled her all night and returned her to the world with love and without mercy. Immediately, she felt the early rigor of the sun, once again slowly sucking the water from her skin, her flesh, and her brain, the water she had won from the luck of the previous day. Then she put her still moist and beating heart back into her chest, stood up, and in obedience to the Cosmos, continued walking.

Two days later, a coyote found her. Furious, he muttered that the business wasn't worth it anymore. He muttered and spat tobacco. Guadalupe walked alongside him and the promise that her agony had ended. The coyote complained several times about the merchandise. The land was no good, it was dry, the fire rose through the stones. The jimadores didn't pay.

So far that season, he had handled nineteen Mexicans, eight Hondurans, five Salvadorans, two Colombians, and someone from further south, a crazy Chilean or Argentine in search of thrills. Almost all of them were short, with broad backs, square heads, and mouths like stone. Few words and much hunger and distrust. He had fed them, and one day, upon returning, he found only the empty house.

The house stood at the foot of a ravine as red as the blood of a quetzal. Inside, it smelled of loneliness and beer. Given its size, it didn't seem like it could have been the refuge for so many people.

Guadalupe's comment didn't sit well with him. At least it was cool shade.

—Guadalupe —he said, smiling— what brings you to the States?

—Necessity brought me, sir.

—Necessity is a serious thing —he said, and with skill, he covered her mouth.

Her eyes swelled with tears and terror. The young blonde had lips as soft as honey. Her eyes were dark but clear. How to put it? Her breathing was agitated but without wrinkles. Like the breath of pleasure, though she didn't understand it that way. The useless little cries, more soft than irritating. That's why she was saved, because I can't stand it when they don't recognize good work in the end. I'd had so many shapeless women that I wasn't going to deny myself that little angel sent from heaven.

Lupita cried all night, but it was hard to say what kind of crying it was. Murmurs. She called for her mother and for someone named "chiquito," who must have been the child she'd left on the other side. They're worse than dogs. Dogs don't leave their puppies.

In the end, I got tired of so much melancholy, and the next day I cut a little lock of her hair and let her go back the way she'd come.

She stumbled away among the stones, as if I might regret it, as if I were incapable of keeping my word. She left sniffling like a child. It seemed more like a cold. The flu. She grabbed her things and left. Crying, of course, like a Magdalene. And the truth is, I regretted it soon after. That girl needed someone to protect her, and I needed someone like her, a butterfly flirting among the flames of the fire, live and in person, not lying down every night with her lovely memory. Who knows if I have a child out there and don't know it. Or a daughter.

Who knows if in fifteen years I'll run into her, light as a little bird, blonde and pretty, just like Lupita was.

Poor life, that of a coyote.

Saturday, June 14. Dow Jones: 12,307
Escondido, California. 5:10 PM

In this country that is one country and many countries, in this people that is one people and many peoples, you will never be in one precise place nor will you be one concrete individual but rather many places and many individuals. You'll sit in a Mexican restaurant and rest your elbows on that long table with tiles that seem handmade in the Zócalo or in Seville, with walls that look painted by a unique artist for a unique place. From none of these details will you be able to tell if you're in Amarillo, Texas, or El Cajon, California, or Bonita Springs, Florida, or Rio Grande, New Jersey. The tables with typical Mexican or Seville tiles will be the same, which is the same as saying they'll be the same tables. And so will the smells and the paintings and the ceramic floors and the view through the window and the girl who will appear and smile at you. It will always be that same smile that comes included in the same menu and at the same price, and you won't mind because you'll know you're paying for her to smile at you, kind, pretty, almost as if she liked you. As if she knew you. Because deep down, she already knows you. She's smiled at you before in other faces like yours, which to her is the same face. And deep down, you'll know it's not sincere, but she doesn't know it, and you won't care either. Because for long faces, there are the government office workers, who also get paid but outside the happy circle of the system, as you'll call it if your name is Ernesto. And if you go twice, three times, five times to the same place, the very same one, you'll find the same tacos and the same tortillas with spicy salsa and the same fajitas and the same margarita and a similar girl with a similar smile, for the same price. But the girl won't be the same either, even though it's the same to say she's the same girl. Because here everything is in motion. Everything is always new even if it's the same. Everything flows like a river that repeats itself at every sunset. But you'll never drive twice on the same highway. The cars will be different and they'll be the same. You'll never pass through the same *self-service* even if the same self-service with the same Indian and the same Hispanics buying the same non-alcoholic beers are in many other parts of many other states. Everything will flow like a *road movie,* everything will be another place and it will be the same. Others will be the girls with blue smiles and the bald old men in office suits and the cheerful old women with short hair and executive strides. And they will be the same. Everything will move without stopping and nothing will change, as if you could get lost in your own home. And with a certain pleasure, you will wander through Virginia and Texas and Arizona and California and rest in all their hotels and motels that, for the same price, will be the same room and the same bathroom and the same lights over a more or less identical parking lot, the same freshly cut grass and the same recently transplanted flowers. And almost with pleasure, you will live fleeing from something, from someone, and from yourself, because fleeing and getting lost is the only form of freedom you will know here. And you will feel like no one and you will feel like everyone, and you will call yourself Ernesto or Guadalupe, José María or María José, and you will be a little of each and you will be the same one who now eats at a *Chili's* in Nevada and at an *On the Border* in Georgia, and you will have the same dreams for the same price and the same fears for the same legal status, and the same ideas from the same education. And you will be an outcast from your country and a persecuted one in this one, if you were poor. Or they won't persecute you, and you will be an exile with some privileges if you earned a university degree before coming. But you will always be a beaten one, resentful of the worst fate of your brothers and sisters whom you don't know. Those brothers to whom you are connected by so many things and sometimes only by a language. And in any case, you will suffer for being an *outsider* who has learned to enjoy that way of being no one, of getting lost in an anonymous labyrinth of restaurants, motels, markets, plazas, distant beaches, mountains without fences, deserts without limits, times of memory without space, countries within other countries, worlds within other worlds. And you will flee without ever returning, but in the end, you will always flee toward the memory that awaits you in every solitude filled with so many people you will never know even if they sleep beside you. And you will only have one safe homeland, but it will be intangible like the wind. You will only have one homeland, one refuge made of fantastic memories about the deep roots of Spanish and the shifting sands of other customs.

Tuesday, June 17. Dow Jones: 12,114
Pueblo, Colorado. 11:52 PM

To think that, just as I have this man in front of me, I once had six of them together. The Devil knows how they understood my order, as they knelt down while murmuring *hala-halas* in fear. The problem came later, when one started to raise his voice and the others followed with their laments, or prayers, the Devil knows what crap they were saying in that demonic language. I would have kept them like that all day, while waiting for reinforcements, but they wouldn't shut up, and that was starting to make me nervous. Then I noticed someone approaching like a shadow. From the length and thinness of the shadow, I realized it wasn't reinforcements but one of those starving dogs. So I had no choice but to shoot. It was my life or theirs. And then the other terrorists who jumped like ghosts wrapped in their white robes, and I had no other choice.

The boys understood. They came in pointing their guns at me, and I could do nothing. I could only wait for them to recognize me by my uniform.

—What happened here? —said Gonsales.

—What do you think happened, you idiot —I said first— Can't you see they almost killed me, and you took forever to get here?

The others, whose names I don't know nor care to know now, inspected the place. The wall was decorated with blood, and the red dirt floor was beginning to absorb the same. The three were leaning against each other, in their white and dirty robes, their eyes staring in surprise toward eternity. Their empty but clenched hands revealed the natural horror in those people.

—It's true —said one, the tallest—; they almost killed him.

—*Sir, your change!* —said the cashier.

I didn't like the tone. Does he think I'm an idiot? He doesn't know I risked my life for him and his whole family, and that's why he speaks to me with arrogance. Imbecile.

But he's going to listen to me, as soon as he gets out of his miserable cashier job.

Wednesday, June 18. Dow Jones: 12,029
Boca Raton, Florida. 11:52 PM

Susana, according to *El País* from Madrid on April 13, a group of Spanish researchers concluded that the extinction of the Neanderthals more than twenty thousand years ago —those gnomes and big-nosed dwarfs that populate the traditional tales of Europe— was due to a fundamental inferiority compared to the Cro-Magnons. According to José Carrión from the University of Murcia, our Homo sapiens ancestors possessed a greater symbolic capacity, while Neanderthals were more realistic and therefore inferior as a society. No one would believe in the myths of those ancestors of ours today, yet their usefulness resembles that of Ptolemaic geocentrism, which in its time served to predict eclipses.

And because our species was more imaginative and delusional, it was stronger. And because it was stronger, imaginative, and delusional, we killed them all.

Friday, June 20. Dow Jones: 11,842
La Mirada, California. 4:52 PM

It could be, Ernesto. It's likely that imagination has run dry. I never thought literature would become as popular as consumer society and communications have made it. A while ago, I came to think that the new generations could text while making love. Now I'm convinced they can make love while texting.

I don't know whether to call that delusion or future realism.

Tuesday, July 8. Dow Jones: 11,384
Toledo, Ohio. 7:45 PM
Every Tuesday night, Margaret would arrive with her folders of notes and teaching materials. Every Tuesday night, María José and Ernesto would listen attentively. Margaret was a government social worker who taught parents how to raise their children. These officials pay close attention to Hispanic families because it is well known that they come from a macho and violent culture. The training consisted of a long forty-minute talk, plus a ten-minute educational video and a ten-minute practical demonstration, which added up to an hour at the end of which María José and Ernesto would sign a paper telling the government that the program was working.

On Tuesday the 8th, Ernesto came home from the construction site in a bad mood, fifteen minutes before

Margaret, and had to make Herculean efforts to stay focused on the week's lesson. If it weren't for the fact that he would be seen as a bad father and worse husband, he would have asked to be allowed to lie on the couch for fifteen minutes with a glass of wine. But he resisted. It was his will and also his job to resist, to show the government official and everyone else that he could come home from work exhausted and sometimes humiliated—Ernesto considered any order he had to follow against his will and in silence a humiliation—and still change diapers, wash dishes, and sing at the same time.

But in the final ten minutes of that day, Luisito was more restless than usual. He repeated the same tantrum three times that kids have at that age, screaming at the top of his lungs followed by rolling on the floor, all over a pencil that his father denied him for being dangerous. Ernesto simply said "no," first and "*no!*" after, which led to the specialist's intervention:

—Try not to say no to him. That's the word children hear the most. That's why they reproduce negativity in their behavior.

—What can we do in these cases, Margaret? —asked María José.

—Hug him. You must comfort him. Tell him you love him. Show him he won't lose your love over spilled yogurt. That will develop his self-esteem and his trust in adults.

—See, Ernesto. You always say that parents are educators, not comforters.

Before she finished the sentence, Luisito spilled the yogurt on the carpet, and Ernesto, in another moment of carelessness, told him not to do it again. But he said it with such vehemence that it surprised Margaret.

As a good professional, without losing her calm and soft, almost sensual tone, Margaret explained that what Ernesto had done was an example of a very common mistake among Latino parents.

—What? —asked Ernesto, almost regretful.

—Raising your voice at the child.

—What was I supposed to do?

—In these cases, the Association strongly recommends explaining to the child that yogurt doesn't go on the carpet. In fact, to avoid hurting his sensitivity, you should have approached the child and played with the spilled yogurt. After all, you'll still have to use a stain remover. It's the same work.

—Yes, it sounds very practical, as always. But I don't think it's such a big deal. When he has a boss like mine and a kid like Luisito, he'll know what it's like to live in a world drawn with thick boundaries.

—Mr. Campos —Margaret reasoned calmly, always avoiding eye contact— the child is two years old… He'll have time to learn all that.

—The sooner the better. Besides, I don't think he'd understand an explanation about the inconvenience of spilling yogurt on the carpet every time he's full.

—From your words, I gather your childhood wasn't easy.

—True.

—Did you witness violent scenes in your family home?

—Yes, a few.

—Did your father hit your mother?

—No, not at all. If anything, it was the other way around. But not even that. My mother was a calm woman too.

—Then?

—For example, more than once I had to watch when one of my father's cows died, and he had no choice but to skin it.

—Skin it? What does that mean?

—Remove its hide. He had to cut it open with a knife along the belly, like this, from top to bottom, and skin it carefully to at least save the hide.

—How awful! How old were you?

—Five or six.

—My God! That's enough to traumatize a child. Didn't your father care? What level of education did he have?

—My father had finished high school and that was it. And because of that, he couldn't afford to lose the whole cow. At least that way he could salvage the hide, and since we were in the Pampas, even though he told me to go far away, I could still see him skinning the dead animal from a hundred meters away. And I won't even tell you about when a ranch hand had to kill a pig by stabbing it in the heart. The animal screamed like a pig.

—My God!

—Someone had to do it. Everyone had to eat. What did you eat today?

—Salad. What else do you remember?

—Sometimes the family of the deceased would be around, a pair of pigs that would start mating in front of me. Those things you don't forget.

—How awful! All of that explains the violence.

—Excuse me, what violence?

—The violence in Latin countries.

—However, I'm not a criminal. I've never killed anyone, and I detest all kinds of violence. For example, I can't stand that out of the hundred TV channels I have here, at least ninety are always showing someone being killed, having an eye gouged out, or being shot in the head. Do you want me to show you?

—That's not necessary. But all of that is fiction.

—Sex can also be acted out, and yet it's taboo or considered pornography. If you're not careful, children can see fifteen murders a night. But if two people share a French kiss, it's censored. You can depict a crime, but you can't depict love.

—My pastor always says something very wise. The evil of the world begins when sex is confused with love.

—No, I don't confuse them. But I also don't see them as necessarily incompatible. Or is it not possible for sex and love to be the same thing sometimes? I mean, in such a materialistic world, every now and then it's possible for them to be the same thing, by miracle or coincidence. Even if only in representation. But no, for public morality, sex is never love and is always obscene. So it must be banned and preached against, to forget that evil wasn't born with sex but with the crime against one's neighbor. But to tell you the truth, the pigs in the Pampas taught me not only that sex is something natural, but they also explained to me what my parents didn't know how to explain in a more scientific way. But on TV, when a guy or a beautiful woman—sorry I didn't say "handsome man"; it's not that I'm sexist, it's that I'm heterosexual—when some Adonis or Amazon points a gun at the forehead of some poor soul and blows them away with a transcontinental missile-like shot, neither of them says a single bad word. That's forbidden and carefully controlled.

—Not in Latin countries?

—No. On the TVs in our countries, they curse like crazy.

—Please, Ernesto! —María José complained, noticing the conversation had completely derailed.

—What? Isn't it true? —Ernesto insisted— Over there, people kiss more often than they kill, and women walk around half-naked.

—Part of the macho culture.

—Yes, they walk around half-naked like in all countries where machismo reigns. Except for Muslim women, who, due to their cultural backwardness, dress more modestly. Because machismo doesn't know how to dress women. It either dresses them with too little or too much. Never just right, like in the United States, where women are free.

—You wouldn't deny that machismo reigns in your countries.

—Many things reign. Of course, we all have flaws. In that, I agree with you. We also have problems with street crime, with organized crime, with the organized poverty of the favelas. But in general, we like death, blood, and the excitement of Agatha Christie-style crime or Arnold Schwarzenegger-style killing machines less. At least when we don't have our own cinema. After all, we have to admit that *The Terminator* had very good special effects. A whole science.

—I repeat, all of that is fiction. Our childhood education programs have been in place for years, and in all the models implemented, violence is prohibited, whether it's saying "no," as you've done, or scolding a child for spilling yogurt on the carpet. Children reproduce what they see.

—However, in this house, no one spills yogurt on the carpet, and we don't have the habit of sticking fingers into electrical outlets. To me, it's in the child's nature, and since in nature there are no electrical outlets or carpets to take care of, there's no choice but to educate. And a clear *no* is better than a hesitant *no* with complexes.

—I hope you're not trying to give us lessons. Studies clearly indicate that all forms of violence must be eradicated in a child's education.

—I'm glad. I already told you I don't condone any form of violence. The problem is defining it. It's also violence to make a child believe the world is as soft as a panda bear.

—For years, we've categorized and eradicated every type of violence, and I can tell you that all these plans have been a success.

—How do you deduce that they've been a success?

For brief moments, Margaret seemed annoyed by Ernesto's questioning. Without rushing, she began organizing her papers in the blue folder.

—Many studies conclusively demonstrate it —she replied.

—Since when do those experiments date?

—From the sixties and seventies.

—Let's see, let me see. If my numbers don't fail me, all the soldiers, generals, politicians, and pastors who participated in and supported the last war in Iraq, to mention just one of many, were educated as children using those non-violence methods. How is it that children so far removed from strong words, from the rigor of their parents, from death, and from sex in all its forms are capable of bombing markets and cities full of children? Children like mine, like yours. Do you know how many people have died in Iraq? Over half a million, if we consider Iraqis as people, of course.

—It's different.

—Yes, it's different. Everything is done with the purest language, with perfect grammar. Freedom, democracy, God, civilization. The blood doesn't splatter. The dead don't have grieving relatives. Those young men —with high self-esteem, no doubt—, those young men who go to kill fanatics in other countries think they're in a *video game*. They press a button and don't even have to witness the unpleasant spectacle of what they're doing. And if one of them sees something live and in person, that is, some dismembered body outside the blue and green screen, they send them to prestigious psychologists, programs that have been successful, theories scientifically proven and endorsed by studies from renowned doctors. And those who don't go to war or commit suicide upon return-ing turn to abusing Coca-Cola, at best, or cocaine, at worst. Did you know that this country, with children so well-educated and removed from sex and the violence of saying no, is the world's largest consumer of narcotics? Did you know that in the country where bad words and the occasional beautiful backside on television are prohib-ited, where a glance can be considered sexual harassment —in fact, here no woman can withstand being looked in the eye; when you look at them, they avert their gaze as if they were nuns being courted— nevertheless, and perhaps because of that, this place is full of sexual psychopaths and serial killers? In our backward countries, killers murder because they're beasts. They shoot someone. Serial killing is almost unheard of because it's an invention of the systematic production and reproduction of things. Killers in those backward countries don't calculate, don't press buttons, and eliminate two hundred thousand people in a single day. That's only possible in a country where children are raised under the best psychological theories of non-violence and modesty.

Margaret didn't lose her composure. She held it in so it wouldn't slip away. She glanced at her watch. With great elegance, she said it was getting late. Three minutes late. The parents signed. Margaret confirmed the number of words that Luisito could pronounce. 33. Normal for his age, but if by the next visit he hadn't been able to connect a noun with an adjective, he would have to be referred to a specialist. She gathered her things, gently, and said goodbye with the same smile as always.

But a second after the door closed, she was heard saying:

—*Fuck you.*

Ernesto couldn't tell if the tone was one of contained rage or the same unflappable tone as always. What he was sure of was that Margaret had wanted to be heard. The best opportunity of her life to say a bad word in public.

Saturday, July 19. Dow Jones: 11,496
Valparaiso, Florida. 9:05 PM

Freedom is a utopia in all its known forms. Wait a moment. No, I'm not arguing in favor of the Castro regime when I die laughing hearing about "the freedom of capitalism" that the true capitalists (I mean, those who have the capital to buy the necessary freedom, those who can lobby in Congress, not humble teachers like us), those, they never believed it. That discourse about the freedom of capitalism is a product for export, not for the consumption of those who produce it. And you know I don't consider capitalism the worst system history has birthed. Yes, the most hypocritical, but not the worst. Of course, you'll ask me why we live in the United States. Maybe we live because, as you say, not everything here is capitalism. There are also people who, without being communists, prevent this from being the Wild West, the land of the neo-Tea Party, of dangerous clowns like some Sarah Palin who, with a smile and in the name of the religion of love and freedom, would rip out your heart in the best Aztec style, who in the name of "zero taxes" have the most

powerful army in the world, financed by the miracle produced by the strength of their prayers on Sunday morn-
ings.

Maoism equalized by uniformizing. To our mentality,
that was slavery. But all that madness was done with the
discourse of "the dictatorship of the proletariat." It was a
dictatorship and it wasn't called anything else, although
with the bureaucratization of communist states, only the
dictatorship remained, not the proletariat. The dictatorship of capital, on the other hand, isn't called "the dictatorship of capital." It adopts better names like "democracy," "freedom of the market," and even just "freedom,"
suggesting it's about the freedom of the individual and
humanity. That's why I say capitalism hasn't been the
worst system history has birthed. Yes, the most hypocritical, but not the worst.

Saturday, July 19. Dow Jones: 11,496
Boca Raton, Florida. 11:45 PM
She said she was going to the bathroom, but she went
for María José. She was going to tell her they were leaving,
she was going to ask her who Lucía was. She was furious
but didn't lose her composure. Lucía had been flirting

with Ernesto since they arrived at the house. She was Hispanic, like her. That's exactly why she didn't trust her. At least not in that. It didn't matter how much she had prayed before dinner. She had learned that Latinas are hot and Latinos are irresponsible. They promise and promise until they get it in, and once they're in, they forget what they promised, she had heard somewhere. A wise prejudice.

With agility, María José took her hand and led her down a hallway to another empty room. She didn't turn on the light. She approached a corner free of furniture and told Guadalupe to kneel. Guadalupe felt the carpet on her knees and the smell of fresh paint on the wall. She didn't say anything. She waited for María José to kneel as well, overcoming the difficulty of a miniskirt that was too tight.

—I don't know if we're doing the right thing— said Guadalupe, without conviction.

—Silly girl —was María José's response. She leaned close to her ear and repeated:

—Don't be silly. Just wait and see.

María José took her trembling hand in the darkness and guided one of her fingers to a small hole. Guadalupe felt the hole and looked through it.

On the other side, Lucía stood up to change the channel. Guadalupe understood that her movements were unnecessary, at least if she wasn't courting Ernesto. Then she confirmed it when he said to her:

—You look very pretty, Lucía.

She looked at him as he approached with a smile that formed in her eyes. Then on her lips.

—You too.

—Why don't you have a digital camera for these things? —asked Guadalupe.

—Lupita, Lupita. It's not the same. There's plenty of that everywhere.

—Please no, Ernesto. No, please.

—Do you have cameras in your house?

—Why not?

—A few. It's to watch the kids when I'm at work.

—Please, not here.

Monday, August 11. Dow Jones: 11,782

Amarillo, Texas. 7:30 PM

In a new attempt to prove his theory, Ernesto X selects a political debate he found at the Main Library of the University. He watches the entire speech three times in the projection room. He takes notes as the giant faces illuminate the room and the notebook where he writes. He doesn't miss a detail.

December 9, 2007, 7:00 p.m. ET, University of Miami. A voice announces the First Presidential Forum of the Republican Party in Spanish, mentioning the rules: in the forum, there will be no debate, no dialogue, and no Spanish will be spoken. Another peculiarity: the ideas forum is organized by the powerful Univision network at the University of Miami. The charming María Elena Salinas modulates her voice. The famous journalist Jorge Ramos, with his usual confidence, states:

RAMOS: ...*Hispanic votes could decide who will be the next president of the United States.*

The audience is somewhat excited.

HUNTER: ...*then, many years later in El Salvador, a Republican president, Ronald Reagan, provided a wall to protect them while they had free elections, which brought freedom to that country. They were two different parties, but I'm talking about the party of freedom, the Republican Party...*

The audience begins to get excited. The heat of Miami fills the room.

SALINAS: *Congressman Paul, the same question. The Republican Party has lost ground, only 23 percent of Hispanics support the party. What can be done to regain that ground?*

PAUL: *...both Hispanics and all other Americans are tired, they are in favor of peace, not in favor of war... We are forgetting our needs here by bombing over there... We're supposed to be fiscal conservatives, and we're not. That's why we lost the election last year, because we didn't uphold the principles in favor of peace, freedom, and the United States of America.*

The applause begins to fade. The next question is about language. Romney smiles, with his impeccable black hair and his ear attentive to the wave of voices. He smiles, perhaps calculating.

ROMNEY: *...we are a plural and wonderful society, this statue that you have here on the screen, behind us, this is a light that illuminates the whole world and says, this is an extraordinary land, this is a land that welcomes people from all backgrounds, from all ethnicities...* (Applause) *We are the party of strength and the party of freedom. Thank you.* (Applause)

SALINAS: *Congressman Paul, what would be the practical value of official English?*

PAUL: *...I think those who attack bilingualism are envious, perhaps they feel inferior because they are not able to speak another language...*

SALINAS: *Exactly one week ago today, Venezuela rejected changes to the Constitution...* (Applause interrupts María Elena, who makes some effort to suppress a smile.) *Many believe that President Chávez is a threat to democracy in the region. If you were president, how would you deal with Chávez?*

PAUL: *Well, he's not the easiest person to deal with, but we have to deal with everyone in the world in the same way, with friendship, the opportunity to dialogue, and trade with people...*

Booing interrupts him. Ron Paul, with his tired eyes but a face already weathered by long years as a dissident, insists, unperturbed, perhaps resigned.

PAUL: *...we spoke with Stalin, we spoke with Khrushchev. We spoke with Mao and we've spoken with the entire world, and in fact, we are at a moment when we must even speak with Cuba.*

Now the booing grows like a hurricane over Miami and over the empty room.

PAUL: ...*and travel to Cuba and trade with Cuba. But let me tell you why, why we have problems in Central and South America: because we have been meddling in their internal affairs for so long, we have interfered in their business matters, and we have created the Chávezes of this world, we have created the Castros of this world, by interfering and creating chaos in their countries, and they respond by ousting their established leaders.*

The booing reaches its climax. Miami wants to eat him alive. The civilized rules of the forum force them to remain indifferent as the next candidate, who has clearly heard the voice of the people, steps up.

HUCKABEE: ...*Although Chávez was elected, he was not elected to become a dictator, which is what he has become by suspending constitutional law. My mother used to say: 'If you give someone enough rope, they'll hang themselves,' and I think...*

The crowd has calmed down with these last words.

GIULIANI: *I, by the way, agree with the way King Juan Carlos spoke to Chávez, and I would do the same. (Applause) Much better than what Congressman Paul wants to do... There is a countermovement in Latin America, it's visible in Panama, in Colombia, it can be seen in Mexico. I believe*

President Calderón was elected—not that I'm an expert in Mexican politics—but I think Chávez had something to do with that...

ROMNEY: ...the course that Americans must take is to continue the isolation of Cuba, to keep them isolated, it's not like what Barack Obama, the Democrat, said, that he would personally visit Castro in Cuba...

MCCAIN: I want to congratulate the Venezuelan people for rejecting this attempt by the dictator to make himself dictator for life. I also want to repeat some words from King Juan Carlos: "Why don't you shut up?". ...I'm glad that I have the support of people who advise me and know a lot about these matters... If I were the president of the United States, I would order an investigation... (Applause) into the Cubans who died, those who were thrown off the plane on the orders of Raúl and Fidel Castro, and I would prosecute them if necessary.

RAMOS: A poll reveals that two out of three Hispanics believe the United States should withdraw its troops from Iraq...

HUNTER: ...if you find out what Hispanics think about the Tenth Marine Division and the Cavalry, the results of the poll will be very different from the one you're talking about. (Applaus)

ROMNEY: ...*what we are doing in Iraq is dealing with the protection of the lives of American citizens, here and in different parts of the world, I mean lives everywhere in the world, honesty, and freedom...*

SALINAS: *Thank you. Congressman Paul, of all of you, you have a different point of view.*

PAUL: *Yes, that's right, I have a different point of view because we are not justified in getting involved there, we did not declare war, and I would tell Hispanics that if they think we should come home, my answer is let's come home as soon as possible. I have a different point of view because I respect the Constitution and I listen to the founding fathers who tell us, "stay out of the internal affairs of other nations..."*

THOMSON: ...*The Hispanic community is known for its values. They know that marriage, for example, is between a man and a woman...* (Applause) *They know that the family is the center of society, and with strong families, we have better societies...* (Applause)

PAUL: *The most important thing Hispanics can do, or what all Americans can do, is come together to restore our Constitution and our great country; we have gone astray, and this is not a Hispanic problem, it's an American problem. What we want is for the rule of law to ensure that everyone has opportunities, not only do we have to restore the Constitution, but first we have to read it and understand what it means. To be free in this country once again.*

The shouts follow Ron Paul's words. Ron Paul is not a good politician. He doesn't know how to listen to the voice of the people of Miami. Ruddy is different, Ruddy knows how to do it.

GIULIANI: *Hispanic Americans have already reached a great level in the United States... Something that has been wonderful for us is that Cuban Americans have come here, they have made us better Americans, it made us better Americans.*

ROMNEY:...we are the hope of the world...*And Hispanics are brave and they are free. (Applause)*

RAMOS: *Thank you very much for trusting Univision and thank you so much for participating in this Republican Presidential Forum broadcast exclusively in Spanish by Univision...*

SALINAS: *Of course, the candidates have already spoken, now it's your turn, the voters. So, if you are a U.S. citizen, register and vote, make your vote count.*

Saturday, September 20. Dow Jones: 11,388
San Francisco, California. 5:30 AM

We were having a great time at Lilian's party when he showed up with his two usual friends, Patrick and the other one I can't remember. I asked Lilian if she had invited them, and she just laughed, which in this case meant no, or that she had no choice but to invite them. I had never had any problems with Nacho before, so don't come at me with that animosity or predisposition, much less premeditation.

It hadn't been premeditated. Nacho Washington Sánchez had come to the party with a gift for the girl who was turning fifteen two days later. Her parents had moved the celebration up to coincide with Saturday the 14th as a reward for her good grades.

Nacho Sánchez, Santa Clara, 19, had returned to school at almost twenty, after spending some time at a chicken factory in Georgia. And this time he had come back with the maturity and determination to earn the second-highest grades in his class.

According to his friends' statements to the police, Nacho hadn't gone to the party for Lilian but for Claudia Knickerbacker, the Chilean friend of the birthday girl.

And if he had said goodbye to Miss Wright with a hug and a kiss on the cheek, that didn't mean anything. Or it didn't mean, as George Ramírez was shouting, sexual harassment.

—The thing is, George is speaking less and less Spanish and he forgot or pretends to forget that we Latinos hug and kiss more often than Yankees. The rest is in the head of one of these repressed people who see sex everywhere and try to extract it with hot pliers. It's true that before leaving for the bus stop, Nacho turned around and told him that George was no longer Mexican-American because in Calabazas North he had lost his *Mexican*ness. It wasn't necessary, especially after enduring like a prince the insults George had thrown at him since he left the Wrights' house.

—What insults? Do you remember any?

—That thing he said, that Nacho was a child abuser, that Lilian was still fourteen and that he was going to report him to the police, and he followed him around threatening him with the phone in his hand. Without turning around, Nacho told him, yes, call 911. The others were behind him.

—How many were there?

—Five or six, I don't remember exactly. It was dark, and I was terrified that a fight would break out and we'd all get caught up in it. There were a hundred yards left to reach the bus stop, and the bus was just waiting at the lights on the next block, and George got the idea to shout at him that he wasn't going to call 911 but Immigration. Everyone knew that Nacho's parents were undocumented and hadn't been able to resolve their status since Nacho could remember, so he himself, being a citizen, always avoided running into the police, as if they were going to deport him or throw him in jail for being the child of undocumented immigrants, something he knew was absurd, but it was stronger than him. When his wallet was stolen on the subway to the airport, he didn't report it and preferred to go home and missed his flight to Atlanta. And that's why you could say the worst things to him, and Nacho would always stay in line, chewing on his anger, but he wouldn't raise a hand, even though he had the strength to bend a donkey. Not him, of course, he wasn't illegal, he was a citizen, and the others must have known that. But the others who were behind him, including John, Lilian's older brother, who understood the words "immigration" and "sexual harassment," stood next to George, who stood out because of his size and his white shirt…

—Would you like some water?

—I quickened my pace, saying we were going to miss the bus, and I got on. After that, I didn't know anything else. I only saw through a window that in the distance they had jumped on Nacho, and Barrett was trying uselessly to rescue him from the mob. But Barrett is smaller than me. Then the lights of Guerrero Street and Cesar Chavez, I sat in the back seat with my phone in my hand until I got home. But Nacho never answered any of the messages I left asking him to call me back. Nacho said goodbye like that because he was happy. She had invited him so he could have a chance with Knickerbacker, and in the kitchen while they were serving the *tres leches*, Knickerbacker hadn't said no. She told him they could go out next Saturday, and that had made Nacho very happy, always so self-conscious about his incipient baldness at nineteen, which he thought was reason enough for any pretty girl to reject him. It's not that the Chilean girl was a model, no, but Nacho was blindly in love since he returned to school.

—And you?

—I don't think that warm farewell was because he was happy. They always act like that, they don't respect personal space. They say Latinos are like that, but if they come to this country, they should behave according to the rules of this country. Here, we only shake hands. We're not in Russia for men to go around kissing each other. Especially not kissing a girl like that in front of her parents and all her friends. You're right, her parents didn't complain, but they also didn't say anything when George and his friends went out determined to teach those intruders a lesson. The Wrights are polite, and since they saw that Nacho left without making a scene, they preferred not to intervene. But they surely talked to Lilian afterward because they had a look of exhaustion that was killing them. It was a moral issue. A matter of principles, of values. We couldn't allow anyone to come and disrupt the peace of the party and abuse one of the girls. No, I don't regret it. I did what I had to do to defend the morality of the house. No, it wasn't my house, but it's as if it were. I've been friends with Johnny since middle school. No, we didn't want to kill him, but he brought it on himself. What crime is worse than abusing a girl? He didn't grope her, but that's how they all start. They, you know who I'm talking about. Them! Don't twist my statement, I know my rights. They don't know how to respect personal space and then they lose control. No, my parents were Mexican, but they entered legally and graduated from the University of San Diego. No, no, no… I'm American, sir, don't get it wrong.

Sunday, September 21. Dow Jones: 11,388
Cocoa, Florida. 10:30 AM

A few days ago, a man recommended I read a new book about idiocy. I think it was called *The Return of the Idiot, The Idiot Returns*, or something like that. I told him I had read a similar book ten years ago, titled *Manual of the Perfect Latin American Idiot*.

—What did you think? —the man asked me, squinting his eyes, as if scrutinizing my reaction, measuring the time it took me to respond. I always take a few seconds to answer. I also like to observe the things around me, take a healthy distance, manage the temptation to exercise my freedom, and, kindly, go to hell.

—What did I think? Funny. A famous writer who uses his fists against his colleagues as his main dialectical weapon when he has them within reach said it was a book with a lot of humor, uplifting... I wouldn't go that far. *Funny* is enough. Of course, there are better ones.

—Yes, that was the father of one of the authors, the Nobel laureate Vargas Llosa.

—Mario, he's still called Mario.

—Well, but what did you think of the book? —he insisted anxiously.

Maybe he didn't care about my opinion but his own.

—Someone asked me the same question ten years ago —I recalled—. I thought it deserved to be a *best seller*.

—That's what I was saying. And it was, it was; indeed, it was a *best seller*. You caught on quickly, just like me.

—It wasn't that hard. First of all, it was written by specialists on the subject.

—No doubt —he interrupted, with contagious enthusiasm.

—Who better to write about idiocy, if not? Second, the authors are staunch defenders of the market, above all else. I sell, I consume, therefore I am. What other merit can there be than turning a book into a bestseller? If it were an excellent book with few sales, it would be a contradiction. I suppose for the publisher it's not a contradiction either that so many books were sold in the Idiot

Continent, right? In the intelligent and successful countries, it didn't have the same reception.

For some reason, the man with the red tie noticed some doubts on my part about the virtues of his favorite books. For him, that meant a declaration of war or something like that. I made a friendly gesture to say goodbye, but he didn't allow me to place my hand on his shoulder.

—You must be one of those who defend those idiotic ideas they talk about in these books. It's incredible that a cultured and educated man like you would hold onto such nonsense.

—Could it be that studying and researching too much are harmful? —I asked.

—No, studying isn't harmful, of course not. The problem is that you're disconnected from reality, you don't know what it's like to live as a construction worker or a company manager, like us.

—Yet, there are construction workers and company managers who think radically differently from you. Could it be that there's another factor? For example, could it be that those who share your ideas are more intelligent?

—Ah, yes, that must be it...

His euphoria had reached its peak. I was going to leave him with that little vanity, but I couldn't hold back. I thought out loud:

—It's still strange. Intelligent people don't need idiots like me to realize such obvious things, do they?

—Negative, sir, negative.

Tuesday, September 23. Dow Jones: 11,010
San Antonio, Texas. 11:05 PM

Lupita was always a girl forced to mature through hardship. But even then, she never fully matured, and I didn't want her to. She was so lovely and affectionate just as she was. Her entire childhood of hunger and her adolescence of screams and humiliations hadn't made her tougher, more resistant to the fate life had dealt her, but quite the opposite. To me, it seemed the old man treated her so badly because Lupita's mother had died in childbirth, and he never forgave her for that.

Who knows if she would have survived the streets of the slum where I took her to save her from the old man's alcoholism. Who knows if she would have had a better life among the streets of New York. Who knows if she would have come if I hadn't painted such a rosy picture of the other side. Don't suffer anymore, Lupita, you can't live like this, half in tears. I'm leaving for Yankee land, and whatever happens, happens. After all, who's going to know we have a photo of Che in the kitchen? We'll take it down tomorrow and put on our best smiles at the embassy.

—They're not going to give a visa to two poor folks like us, Nacho. We don't even have enough to eat.

—No one knows that, not your father or your sister. Certainly not my poor old mother, who's half-blind. You'll follow me later.

I'm not going to stand you leaving, she told me, and I said we wouldn't be apart for long.

—How long is not long? A year? Two years?

—No, not that long. It'll be a few months. As soon as I can save enough for your plane ticket, you'll come.

Back then, they didn't deny visas like they do now. Besides, Lupita had a translator's degree, though in the two years we lived together in the slum, she did two jobs and only got paid for one because I had to go in person to throw my weight around. And after they stole our TV and the Teflon pots Lupita's sister had given us, and luckily we weren't in the shack that Saturday, I told her I was leaving in February.

We spent the whole Sunday staring at the ceiling, watching the zinc sheet sweat from the sheer humid heat that wouldn't let us sleep. But it wasn't the heat, it was this life we'd been dealt, and no man could change it, and if I'd known, I wouldn't have come into this world under these conditions.

And when are we going to have a child like this? she started, and I said nothing, nothing at all because I had nothing to say. I thought that if she hadn't been more miserable with her father, I would never have taken her from her home. At least there they had a ceiling and the neighbor's dog barking at her from the rooftop, and the roof didn't sweat in the summer, and there was no shortage of bread and pasta on Sundays and the sad stories from the old Italian man before the heat of the sauce and the steam of the red wine went to his head. Sure, even though there were plenty of fights and shouts, damn those people. Dad, have a coffee, a coffee please, Dad, Nacho's here today. What Nacho, don't tell me what to do in my own house, can you believe it? Make your man some coffee so he doesn't run off, and I'll have to put up with another lazy bum like this one. Another what, Dad, if I only had two boyfriends. Look, don't make me talk. Why Don Paolo? What does he have to say that I don't know? Two that I know of, the old man would say, and he'd start getting worked up. And me, out of some macho complex, wanted to know how many boyfriends Lupita had had. Lupita's no saint. Like ten, or maybe eleven, the neighborhood soccer team. Don't say that, Dad, you know it's not true, don't be mean. Mean? I didn't even count the substitutes. And then I'd tease Lupita about that one official boyfriend she'd had, and she'd defend herself by saying I knew she was a virgin when we met and other things that aren't even worth bringing up now.

The heart is blind, I'd tell Lupita. Otherwise, the eyes wouldn't be in the head; they'd be in the chest. If I hadn't fallen in love, I wouldn't have left the old lady's house either. But there are things you can't choose. I fell in love, and I could never stop loving Lupita, like a sick man, I couldn't.

I thought about all that while staring at the sweaty ceiling, and it didn't get me anywhere. Then she'd get sadder because I didn't want to talk. But I never stopped thinking and thinking. That's what I remember most from that time. I spent my days thinking, calculating, imagining, fantasizing for nothing.

Until last February, when the club's youth team went on the long-awaited tour to Los Angeles, and one night there, after the game we tied two-two, with a terrible performance on my left wing, I disappeared. I left the pit, as the guys from school used to say. They say the coach looked for me but didn't get too worked up about it. Besides, he knew I was a hack and had no future in the club. Not in that one or any other. And since I wasn't Cuban either, no one noticed. Later, I stayed quiet when a Mexican gave me a gig at his restaurant in Santa Monica.

It took me two days to get a job, and Lupita wrote to me saying how wonderful, how wonderful, Nacho, now we'll finally be able to live our lives in peace.

For me, at first, that was paradise. Reading Lupita's emails so happy, even though she couldn't sleep at night because of the fear in the slum. But she had so much hope and kept talking about the child we didn't have yet, saying we shouldn't be negative, that things worked better that way. So I exaggerated all the good things here or didn't mention that one day I'd run into a gang, a crew as they call it there, and had to hand over all the week's money.

CRISIS

Don't open your mouth, a Panamanian friend told me. They'll mistake you for an American because of your hair and eyes, but as soon as you say something, they'll figure out you're illegal and you're paid in cash, and they'll follow you and leave you without a dollar, in the best-case scenario.

But little by little, everything changed. In two months, I'd saved enough for Lupita's ticket, but then the crisis hit, and I was the first to go before the restaurant closed, because I was the new guy, they said. Still, I sent the money to Lupita so she could come, because we couldn't take it anymore. I didn't think it would be so hard to find work later.

With Lupita, we looked for work in Los Angeles and then in Las Vegas and then all over Arizona until we ended up in San Antonio, with the promise of a Puerto Rican who had a cleaning company. The truth is, cleaning hotels and offices wasn't as easy as it seemed at first. The boss was always unhappy with our work. If it wasn't too slow, it was too careless. I started to think he was messing with us, or we just didn't understand what he wanted, and two weeks later, we were back on the street.

Literally on the street, because we had to wait on a corner in the early morning because that's where they picked up undocumented workers. And me and Lupita there, in the middle of all these men who, luckily, didn't treat us badly, quite the opposite, but the truth is, I always had Jesus on my lips and was looking around to see who might mess with Lupita. So much so that in this job, I didn't pay attention to the trucks that passed by and picked up workers. The Mexicans were the most skilled at this, and I had to watch and learn from them. Sometimes Lupita would ask me why I didn't approach the guy in the white truck, the one in the black car, who seemed to have good work, but the truth is, I didn't want to leave her there alone, waiting, before it was fully light, so I'd act distracted or say that one wasn't right for us for this or that reason.

Until a black SUV passed by and signaled to someone, and he came to tell me they wanted the girl. I went up to the truck, and the guy with the sunglasses at that time of day didn't inspire much confidence. He had work for maids in a wealthy family's home, he said, but in the back, I didn't see any other women. Lupita, paler than usual and with trembling lips, told me we couldn't let another opportunity slip by because we wouldn't have anything to eat.

I didn't say anything, but she ended up getting in the back, surely against her own will. And when the truck started moving, she waved at me with her little hand and blew me a sad kiss. I knew she was crying because I know her. I knew this wasn't going to work, and this damn life wasn't going to work either.

Wednesday, October 15. Dow Jones: 9,301
El Dorado, Kansas. 9:10 AM

If I were a painter, Ernesto thought, I'd paint cubes, abstract prisms on black grids. Nothing abstract. That's this country. Containers surrounded by seas of parking lots. Only the Black and Latino people sit outside to watch time and people pass by. The white people hide in their livings and their dyings. At most, in the summer, they go out to their backyards, where no one sees them. That is, if they don't go inside, they go backward. And to disguise or soften that closed-off nature, they leave the front windows open, perfectly lit, so that those passing by can see each of the main rooms, their paintings, their furniture, their fine lamps. All empty, of course, all uninhabited, because one thing is to open up and show the perfection of such private museums, and another is to let yourself be seen.

Later, when they die, they go out into public space. Their cemeteries are beautiful, open parks, without walls or fences. Walking distractedly—supposing someone is walking—one might come across a collection of tombstones surrounded by grass and beautiful plants. Tombstones with all that information they keep secret in life so no one steals their identity: name, surname, place and date of birth, last known residence.

Latinos don't; so open to urban space, so much revelry in the streets, but when they die, they shut themselves away in those horrible walled cities no one wants to see.

Anglos sure know how to die.

But they don't know how to live. They don't know how to eat, they don't know how to waste time, they don't know how to talk. From the containers of their homes, they move to the containers of their cars, and from there, even more closed containers await them, surrounded by parking lots, larger black areas gridded with white and yellow where the mobile prisms are placed so drivers can reach the fixed prisms. Like schools and high schools. Blind prisms on blind prisms, surrounded by other prisms without windows or windows that can't be used. The classrooms have no windows, though the prisms are meticulously surrounded by conditioned nature. Except for the cafeterias, except for the recreation rooms. And if they have any opening to the outside, it faces the gridded parking lots. In any case, the gardeners work meticulously. The investment in trees, grass, plants, and flowers is almost as high as the investment in maintaining the parking lots and the containers. To compensate for the scarcity or absence of windows, surveillance cameras point everywhere. The prisms don't look; they watch.

After being released from the containers of education, the young people rush to the containers of supermarkets, which are also containers of education. There, too, the light of natural nature doesn't enter. There are suns that shine inside the containers. Natural time doesn't exist. Only real time exists, which is shopping time. And more black hemispheres hang from the ceilings. They don't look either; they also watch.

From the supermarket containers, from the store containers, they move to the city containers, enormous bazaars, troglodyte cities with stores, pizzerias, restaurants, banks, hair salons, massage parlors, casinos, army recruitment centers, where the light of the outside world barely enters.

The only moment a modern troglodyte knows what nature is, the warmth of the sun, or the humidity of the rain is when they leave the air conditioning of their car and have to walk ten yards to one of these containers. The suffering is minimal because the skin doesn't have time to suffer the rigor of the cold, the heat, it doesn't have time to sweat or contract from the gusts of snow.

Natural nature is a snobbery. Real nature is the one inside the *malls*, it's the corrected, perfected nature. The tropical trees under the snow-laden domes prove it. Their fruits aren't eaten, but they also don't dirty the floor. This way, men and women can rest from shopping and then get back to it. Others take the opportunity to sweat in the *gyms* equipped with machines for running, machines for moving arms, machines for simulating walking to work twice a week, machines for feeling like you're coming back from the supermarket with bags in your hands and all that hassle of reality. Chinese relaxation techniques and Hindu yoga between a watch stand and a rock music stand with Michael Jackson blasting at full volume. Screens with moving chairs so the younger ones can ride horses or play tennis without a ball, without a court, and without the sun bothering their eyes.

Machines to simulate a war that will one day come, with people who don't die, with dead who rise again, with dead made better dead by technology and deaths corrected by science and the culture of good killing. Which is a natural killing and a real killing. Because it's not just the dead who will one day sow the jungles and the deserts in some savage country but the obese dead who walk around sucking on a giant cup of Coca-Cola while with their lost gazes they search for something else to buy.

Wednesday, October 15. Dow Jones: 9,001
Las Cruces, New Mexico. 1:10 PM
"Where are you going?" the officer asked him.

"I'm walking," Ernesto replied.

"Walking?" For a moment, the officer didn't know what to say— "What do you mean *walking*?"

"I'm circling the school. I'm waiting for my son to get out."

"Do you have identification?"

"Of course. Here you go."

"Ernesto Sabatini..." You can't just circle the school like that. There are minors in the building and we must avoid suspicious individuals in the area.

"Suspicious?"

"No one walks around here. Do you see anyone walking?"

"No, no one walks around here, even though there's a beautiful path, which isn't common either."

"That's why you should avoid raising suspicions."

"If I take my car and circle the cube, is that okay?"

"What cube?"

"I mean, the school building."

"Oh, sure, of course. You can drive around freely. Like everyone else."

"But if I walk, I raise suspicions."

"Please return to your car."

"Thank you, officer."

Wednesday, October 15. Dow Jones: 8,577
Orofino, Idaho. 6:30 PM
People don't understand the kindness of the holy little death just because she has that deathly look with the skull and all that, but we venerate her for all the trials she has

put us through in the hardest times, from the harsh days of sun in Sinaloa and the dust in Sonora to when we crossed and came not as wetbacks but rather as dry, parched, and we entrusted ourselves to her every day in the desert where we almost died of cold or fried in the sun or eaten by insects and almost turned into jerky for the coyotes, dried out by the thirst of the land that sucked us up from our heels to wring our heads like a wet rag until we were left without a drop of hope to survive, but the holy death, whom we also feared just to look at as children, took pity on our suffering because all true faith begins with fearing true holiness, and that's how one learns what respect and humility are, which are declared in prayers with the heart, which is why the Saint heard our pleas and remembered the offerings when we crowned her with twenty-dollar bills and even hundred-dollar bills and placed a Marlboro and another special cigarette and even a bit of heavenly powder in the little hole of her nose, which is what the holy little death likes, and which, according to the compadre who survived with me, was the most valuable offering that marked a path for us, so thanks to her powerful intervention, today we can tell the story and no longer have to hide from Cacho's gang or

Chapo's gang from El Paso, and we dedicate ourselves to singing our *narcocorridos*, which are so successful in Texas and New Mexico and Arizona, and they say they're even played on the best radio stations in Los Angeles and danced to by our brothers in Chicago, though, well, it's not the same there in the cold as in the warmth of the land, but the people always keep the traditions and enjoy our little narcocorrido step that we bring to all our Latino brothers so they keep their spirits up and don't get discouraged at the first obstacle and always remember the holy death, who is capable of terrible punishments for those who mock her or criticize her for this and that without knowing, because people judge what they don't know, but she is like a protective mother and never tires of performing true miracles like the ones she did for us, and you can see it right now, live on your prestigious program, giving us so much success and fortune, returning to us in millions what we gave with sincere faith and respectful humility but with conviction, as our lord, may he rest in peace, said, that faith moves mountains and even more so faith in the holy little death if one is able to overcome the prejudices about her appearance, because it's logical that people, or rather many people, still don't understand

and that's why they don't accept that this worship is like any other, only it is based on true evidence of its miracles, and I would tell all those who still do not accept the kindness of the Holy Death that it doesn't matter if the skeletons used to dress and create her image once belonged to a man or a woman killed by narcos or who died just like that, because we will all die someday, and that doesn't mean we become saints, much less a holy virgin, but rather it is the symbolic resource we, the faithful, use to represent the Holy Death, which is something that transcends the materiality of real bones and transcends the materiality of money, cigarettes, and whiskey that she consumes, because all of that represents our material needs, the real needs of the people, to lead a life full of power in her honor and in honor of the Father, and that we, well, right now, are going to sing so that the essence of traditions is not lost and so that we serve as an example to future generations, and all of this is what we wanted to express in our latest hit, "They are looking for him," which refers to Chapito, the son of the leader of the gang that created the "pasito de la muerte,"[1] and who died in a

---

[1] *Pasito de la muerte,* little step of death.

shootout after singing his last narcocorrido in honor of the wrong man and without the protection of the Holy Death, which doesn't mean we sing about drug trafficking as some are saying out there, but rather we sing about things as we see them, things as they are, we sing about the problems of the people who are abandoned, and if the main characters of our songs are men who have been accused of being narcos or who lead organizations outside the law, well, it's because they have objectively shown resilience and leadership skills, and the people recognize them as brave figures beyond the fact that we do not promote the drug trade, but as artists, we make use of the natural gift that the Lord has bestowed upon us and that the Holy Death helped to temper in the most difficult moments of our lives to reveal the path and our personal mission in this world, so I hope all our people enjoy it and feel inspired to keep pushing forward and always moving ahead.

Tuesday, October 21. Dow Jones: 9,033
La Plata, Maryland. 11:50 PM
He had decided to finish those damn graphs in an *Excel*, useless according to him but *as soon as possible* for the

section director, Mr. ASAP. And he had started by down-loading the latest data from the email, and while down-loading, he began reading a message from some useless person, who turned out to be a certain María José who had sent him a link. Maybe it was spam, or maybe he had forgotten about this María José, and at the risk of it being a virus, he clicked on the link that led to YouTube.

A girl of dreams, dressed in an anachronistic long dress, stood waiting in the middle of a television set from the eighties. But when the first note played, he recognized her immediately.

Today, the sun shines through my window,
and my heart grows sad
as I gaze upon the city

What had become of Jeanette's life? For the first time, he discovered the eyes behind that voice that transported him without permission to his early adolescence. Back then, in his town, you could only hear that voice on the radio once in a blue moon. But it was enough to remem-ber her all day and all night. Above all, he remembered her in *Cría cuervos*, that movie he remembers little of, and almost all of that little is her voice as a lonely teenage girl at the station. And now he was falling in love again with those eyes that delve into the soul like the Mediterranean and make the chest feel like on a roller coaster, with that smile, with that innocent teenage hairstyle of someone who dreams but does not yet know love, pain, or apathy. Jeanette, Jeanette, that madness, fantasy, fullness of being alive, and promise of living from when we were young and knew how to truly admire another person, the slow walk of a beautiful girl, always out of reach except when she asked us the time or if the teacher had arrived. And when the miracle happened, it was as if we had been blessed by heaven, rewarded for the long and nervous wait for a glance, for a word from her. Jeanette, now he remembers that lost emotion of admiring and being admired, of falling in love with the untouchable girl who sings and dreams of hearts that gaze in admiration and because of that write, paint, play the piano, and die to get the attention of that young woman I don't want to think will one day be an old lady but rather a pure and eternal little work of art, of "Porque te vas," why are you leaving.

> *I am rebellious*
> *because the world has made me this way*
> *because no one has ever treated me with love*
> *because no one has ever wanted to listen to me*

He was going to look her up on Wikipedia but thought it was better not to know anything more. He just wanted to see her like that. Like that forever. Besides, he had to finish those graphs *Excel* about the 3% advance of the 15% of the pipes that go from the plaza to the new building of Blueman Co. And even though it was past midnight, it was better to do them than to endure the unbearable director ASAP threatening with another round of layoffs. Because the question isn't whether there will be layoffs, but when and who. And for him, being fired would mean losing his legal status, being expelled from the country, returning to that land of Jeanette that no longer exists. Which is a thousand times worse than making those thousand times cursed and useless graphs, which don't help advance the work on the pipes nor do they provide a statistic that would be useful for the next project, but only to keep his employees under control. Control, control, even when it's time to dream.

>*and I wish I could be like that boy*
>*like that man who is happy*

Then he thought that there are two parts to life. One is the real one, the other is the fictional one. The real one is what we once imagined. The fictional one is the routine wrapped in obligations, deceptions, and disillusionments.

and I wish I could give what's inside me
everything in exchange for a friendship
and to dream, and to live...

Friday, November 28. Dow Jones: 8,810
Fort Salonga, New York. 3:15 PM

Who knows if they'll catch us. José, I don't think so, because the guy's illegal, he doesn't exist. But they might recognize me from the Wal Mart cameras. I've been going to that Wal Mart for about ten years. I always told Olga that I loved it for the prices they have there and which, by the way, helped me survive when I first came here and worked at a General Dollar for six hundred pesos a month.

I got into this Black Friday thing about two years ago. The first time out of curiosity. Then because I realized the advantage of buying a truckload of stuff at clearance prices. Last week it was because of the crisis. Yeah, because of the crisis we're in. It's not like I had anything specific in mind when I went, just that you always find bargain prices. José was going for a new iPod and a Bluetooth.

And we were there from four in the morning, freezing in a line a hundred yards long because if we stayed in the car with the heater on, it was like staying at home to arrive last. That's why, I think, when people saw movement inside the store, they started getting impatient.

After that, I don't remember much. I just remember the line started moving like a river resuming its natural course. The current dragged us along, and we pushed too, we weren't going to fall behind. People were shouting and laughing. I saw José laughing like crazy and making me laugh too. So with all the laughter, we didn't even feel that they were hitting us hard on the back, nor did we feel that the soft thing we stepped on was a guy, the employee who was crushed to death. I only remember that José found his iPod and his Bluetooth at half the price they sell for at Best Buy. And then this, I find myself stuck at home, hardly going out, and Olga asks me what's wrong and I say nothing, as usual, wiped out from work. And she keeps insisting on going shopping, and I'm hurting here and there.

Every now and then I turn on CNN, search the internet to see if there's anything new, call José who now with his Bluetooth talks less and less, or doesn't want to talk about anything other than the advantages of having a

Bluetooth. It must be to avoid talking about the guy we crushed at Wal Mart. I wonder if we're at fault, or if the guilt divided into a hundred parts is the same guilt a real killer might have. I've never killed anyone, though I've come close a few times to being finished off myself.

The blame lies with these big stores. They're always open twenty-four hours, but on Black Fridays they close them to keep the shoppers from invading. Have you ever seen such insanity?

I'd rather think that if there's no news saying it was my big-footed stomps that killed the Wal Mart employee, then it wasn't me, I'm not the guilty one of homicide. In fact, what must have happened is that the soft thing that was complaining wasn't even a person. The other day I saw a tiger-shaped cushion that hugs you and is good for watching TV, and I think it even roars like a person, like a woman. And it hugs you so you don't feel alone.

Monday, December 1st. Dow Jones: 8,149
Aurora, Illinois. 10:15 PM

Statistics show that suicide is the most traumatic family event, and in many cases, attempts end in failure, leaving even more severe consequences for the individual. The arts do not recommend it. The sciences do not promote it. Law and morality question it. Most religions condemn it. In case you decide to use our services, any legal claim will fall on the company. We guarantee the best service and the most humane treatment for your problems. You choose the payment method and the method of execution. Firearm, bladed weapon, accident, or poisoning. You can choose the genre. Hero, martyr, patriot, misunderstood, criminal, or distracted. Prices vary based on the popularity of the genre and the pre-scene preparations. In all cases, we ensure efficiency and absence of pain. If you are not satisfied, we will refund your money. But remember, when life requires definitive solutions, we are here to help you.

Tuesday, December 2nd. Dow Jones: 8,230
La Grande, Oregon. 6:50 PM

Tony González was watching ABC News and stroking his right thigh. The president was giving one of his last interviews as president. Since Tony returned from the war, he's been like this—I don't know if I'd say pensive or if he just doesn't want to think about what happened or talk about it. But he's proud of having served his country, and I do what I can to keep him from changing his mind. General Patrik González himself, what a coincidence, almost sharing his last name, pinned the Silver Star for valor on him. He's very proud of that decoration, earned with just merit. But he got angry one day when he heard me tell María José that I didn't understand why they hadn't given him the Gold Star, since he risked his life to save five fellow soldiers from certain death. The crazy María José, who's a bitter liberal, according to Tony, had said or suggested, I don't even remember, that if he weren't Latino, he would have received the Gold Star. Last night I had to call María José to tell her not to come back. The crazy woman came at me with some speech or other, the kind those irresponsible people from San Francisco always have, and I hung up on her. So, one less friend.

Tony had thrown himself on a poorly made grenade to protect his comrades. The command decided to give him the Silver Star, and Tony thanked them with tears because the words wouldn't come out then.

"I think I was unprepared for war."

Tony looks at that face a fellow soldier had stuck on a wall. The face says it wasn't prepared for war. The face smiles, wrinkles, turns red, smiles again with obviousness:

"The biggest regret of all the presidency has to have been the intelligence failure in Iraq"—says President George Bush, smiling with the right side of his mouth.

He was a great president, just unlucky. The war, the economic crisis that left Tony with no job prospects. Even less so in his condition, María José said, even less so, the way he is, sad all day, waiting to be told again that he risked his life for his country and for the freedom of the world.

"A lot of people put their reputations on the line and said the weapons of mass destruction is a reason to remove Saddam Hussein. It wasn't just people in my administration; a lot of members in Congress, prior to my arrival in Washington D.C., during the debate on Iraq, a lot of leaders of nations around the world were all looking at the same intelligence."

With a finger, he presses his temple, as if searching there for some explanation for his inexplicable sadness.

"And, you know, that's not a do-over, but I wish the intelligence had been different, I guess."

The nation honors him, but he is sad. On one wall is Tony in a bed and the president who visited him two years ago. He had said, the president had said, that he would never forget Tony's sacrifice. And David had told him that the president was a man of his word. But Tony had waited hours, days, months for that interview with the president and knew the president would remember him again. It's just that the journalist kept insisting on other things.

"I think I was unprepared for war."

Tony *I wish* stroked the stump *the intelligence* on his right. For some reason *had been different* he still felt his leg there, *I guess* moving like a ghost. *I think* Also *I was* he was missing the other leg, but *unprepared* he didn't feel it there, it was as if it were asleep *for war*.

Tuesday, December 2nd. Dow Jones: 8,230

Espanola, New Mexico. 9:16 PM

Although I'm a staunch pacifist, I must admit that my life, our lives, and the lives of all those who haven't yet died depend on the sacrifice and death of some other living being. Even a vegetarian must kill to live, if not the vegetables they eat, then the trees they cut down to build their house. These deaths can always be justified. We can say that plants don't feel pain or that they don't have emotions. Carnivores can argue the same: lower animals aren't rational or don't know what they're doing or what is being done to them. And so can abortionists and common criminals and even the justice system. There's always a good reason to kill. One way or another, we're alive because some other living being has died, because they continue to die, surrendering their right to life in our favor.

The biggest problem with these kinds of truths is that they're very useful to hypocrites. Like many other truths fragmented by power.

Tuesday, December 23rd. Dow Jones: 8,419
Primos, Pennsylvania. 6:15 PM

Guadalupe had never known a cold like the one in Philadelphia. At the bus stop, she huddled, trying to cover her son's little body with her own. But the shelter was barely like a piece of transparent eggshell, and the wind crept in from below and swirled above. The bus hadn't come yet and probably wouldn't. Either Guadalupe didn't know that it never came after six or she thought it had broken down on the way. She hadn't imagined it would already be dark at that hour; otherwise, she would have brought the fur coat José had given her on her last birthday in Arizona.

When it was already dark, a car passed by and stopped. A voice from inside called her name, but Guadalupe didn't answer. It shouted again for her to get in the car, but Guadalupe didn't answer. So the car's tires screeched on the asphalt, and it sped away.

"Don't be scared, baby," Guadalupe said slowly, "don't be startled, my little one."

The child fell back asleep.

The mother's purple fingers stroked the child's blond hair.

"Blondie," José had said, how is it possible that the kid is blond if there are no blondes in the family? Don't be stupid, Nacho had told him, all kids are born with eyes that light. You're just a kid without children who doesn't know anything about that, José had shouted. Don't you dare try to educate me. Don't be crazy, José, just because you're a father doesn't make you wiser. They say you're not a pianist just because you have a piano. That remains to be seen, so shut up and finish that dough or the boss will fire us both. That's how you're going to repay me for getting you the job.

As if these newcomers are going to educate me. Latino parents and a blond kid like a Yankee. And even if it's true that Machito's hair and eyes got darker over time, he's still blond. His hair is like Sofía's, that little Argentine girl who drove us crazy at Taco Bell. Fine, blond hair. What does Machito have of the Reyes family? Nothing. Lupe defends herself by saying one of her grandmothers was blond. But the old lady died before Lupe even realized she had a blond, blue-eyed grandmother. What a coincidence, huh? If it's not a lie from Lupe, it's a lie from her mother, famous in San Salvador for making things up. Maybe the blond Indian existed, but she just had to ruin my life. I had to ask Chapo, who knows computers, to retouch some photos of Machito, make them darker or something, fix them to send to the family. Let's see if they leave me alone then. They already have enough with the money I send them, I don't know what else they want.

José Reyes turned right and headed back to the stop where Guadalupe was.

"The fool doesn't know there are no buses at this hour."

But before arriving, he knew Guadalupe wouldn't agree to get in the car. He stopped, turned off the radio, sat for a moment in thought, and finally decided not to go there. He couldn't handle another snub from Lupe. Let's see if she learns not to play hard to get.

He took the highway to Camden. As he crossed the New Jersey bridge, it began to snow. During the two years they were in Arizona, Guadalupe had hoped it would snow. She had never seen snow in her life. In Arizona, there's no snow, Guadalupe, that's why it's called Arizona and not Nevada. But Guadalupe had seen postcards of the Grand Canyon in winter. That's far from here, Guadalupe, maybe we can go next year. We couldn't go because there was never any time, her scrubbing the floors at the Radisson and me busy making tacos and pizza. And when I lost my job in a raid, we fled to the north. On the Greyhound, she told me she was going to see the snow. And she was right, we couldn't escape that one.

José turned the windshield wipers to full speed. Snow at sixty miles per hour is like a trip to the stars in one of those ridiculous movies where the stars pass by the spaceship. More like entering a tunnel, or swimming through a school of fish in the Caribbean.

But colder, much colder, José thought. Everything is colder here. Cold like the cold blondes of the north.

Tuesday, December 23rd. Dow Jones: 8,419
Los Altos, California. 9:15 PM

Susana, to distinguish a novel from a critical study, your colleagues call the former "creative literature." It doesn't matter that, as a rule, what they call *novel, short story* or *drama* is the application of skills and interests in service of a publishing market. They call *creative literature* the least creative literary genre of all. After the brevity of the avant-garde, if a novel doesn't respect a minimum of the conservative spirit that guides the tastes of critics and especially the tastes of consumers, no one or almost no one will read it. Or am I wrong? At best, it will end up on the honorable shelf of the rare. Then, the academics who live parasitically off *creative literature* will consider it a subgenre, the product of unserious people who don't know what they're doing. Geniuses thus become like children whose drawings are analyzed by their parents or psychologists with the theory of the moment.

But our world is the world of masks. The country with the best universities and the most Nobel Prizes is a moderately ignorant country that doesn't know the number of its own population, let alone any serious fact about another country. Not even when they're at war with that other country. The country with the most gold medals in athletics is the country that lives in cars, the country with the most obese and super obese people in the world. The country known for its elegant movie stars is the country where women have no sense of elegance. There, women crowd clothing stores and buy everything that's in fashion. But they don't wear clothes; they consume them. They put on clothes like someone eating at a *fast food* joint. The country that most cares about and censors bad language, the country where a glance into someone's eyes can be considered sexual harassment, is the country that exports the most pornography in the world. The country where civil laws are most respected is the country that most violates international laws. *And so forth and so on.*

That's why all their fantasy heroes wear masks or hide something terrible or something powerful, an accident that turns them into monsters, almost always good ones. Monsters who fight for justice or are going to save the world from the normal bad guys. Because it had to be an empire, Susana, born from its contradictions, the producer of heroes who fight for justice and freedom. Before, at least, empires were proud to be empires. But the Americans invented cinema, real fiction, and the simulacrum.

Speak softly and carry a big stick, said Theodore Roosevelt. Because everything is, or can be, its exact opposite.

Look at the characters of Walt Disney and Hanna Barbera. They are all the more real the more hybrid they are. The central protagonists of this world, like Mickey Mouse or Donald Duck or Tom and Jerry, are anthropomorphized animals. But this central nature is surrounded and framed by secondary beings: real animals or real humans. The humans almost always appear from the waist down. They are recognized by their feet and their clumsiness (Mammy Two Shoes). Even when they are seen, their faces are not the faces of gods but of clueless, foolish, naive beings in the face of the cunning of the hybrid beings. Similarly, some animals appear in their animal state. These also don't have a central role or full awareness of what is happening at the center of the plot. They are almost always dogs (Spike, Pluto).

Here a new unfolding occurs, as you say. In the "real world" of humans, dogs represent authority, reliability, friendship, and above all, loyalty. For this reason, when entering the "real world of fiction," we see that dogs generally take on roles as guards and police officers. Not without paradox, these roles do not represent cunning but rather naivety. The law is naive; crime is cunning. Nevertheless, the "naivety of the guardian" remains a positive ethical value.

On the other hand, cats, symbols of independence and unpredictability in the "real world" of humans, are maintained in the form of illegality. The dog-cat opposition, with their represented values of loyalty-infidelity, persists, but the protagonism, the quasi-sympathetic monopoly, belongs to cats and their pursued, the mice.

Mice, for their part, share the center of the "real world of fiction" with cats. They are all the more real the more hybrid they are. The temporary alliances between mice and dogs are achieved through the cunning of the mouse, not the dog, in this way gaining security and protection against the pursuit of the cat. Thanks to this protection, the mouse acts with impunity, mocking the cat.

Now, Susana, if we return to the "real world of humans" on the global stage, the alliances hardly vary: Spike, the guardian dog who holds the legal and uncontested power, is the center of the empire—in this case, the United States; Tom, the cats, are the governments or forces opposed to that dog's order, while Jerry, the mice, are the weak dissidents who must rely on political deceit to survive the tyranny of the cats.

The duality is not shown in the power of the dog, Spike, nor in the naivety of the people, Mammy Two Shoes, but in the cat and the mouse, who are alternately good and bad, sometimes repressive dictatorships against dissident victims and other times friendly dictatorships against guerrilla criminals. The viewer knows or perceives that the mouse is both the victim and the provocation of disorder.

The hegemonic power—the guardian dog—is presented with an attribute contrary to reality, naivety and goodness, defense instead of aggression. On the other hand, the instruments of that power, the second tiers of the hierarchy, are the repositories of all the evil of a secondary force. This model has been repeated throughout history. In imperial Spain, from the political essays of Quevedo (*Política de Dios*), the fictional literature of Cervantes (*Don Quixote*), the theater of Lope de Vega (*Fuente Ovejuna*) to the denunciations of Bartolomé de las Casas (*Destruction of the Indies*) and the chronicles of Guamán Poma de Ayala (*New Chronicle and Good Government*), what was considered the highest political and moral power, the kings, are never called into question in the face of a complaint. In fact, all complaints about violations, oppressions, injustices, and exploitations are directed at the kings as complaints against the viceroys or governors. Big Brother is the oppressor and the security to which the victim turns. The history of the United States' war of independence is no different. Even in the famous *Common Sense* by Thomas Paine, all the arguments and probably all the intentions of the Americans rising in rebellion against the British Empire were not directed at King George III but at the middle ranks of the hierarchical structure: parliament and its ministers. In fact, the idea of independence was not dominant until the publication of the 46 pages by the radical Englishman, which had nothing of "common sense" for the overwhelming majority of Americans of his time.

The kings—the dogs, Big Brother—represented a legal, legitimate, and rather naive power. The middle ranks, the ministers and governors, the tax collectors were the true cats.

But you know that power, Susana, needs to practice a permanent travesty since its strength always lies in its invisibility. In the nineties, *The Simpsons* made an important variation by avoiding animal hybridism and presenting the "real world of humans" without the expected doubling, thus becoming an example of criticism from the very instruments of previous dissemination. In this sense, they resemble and surpass The Flintstones. However, by resorting to entertainment, they neutralize any possible criticism, turning a potential real drama into an undoubted fantastic comedy. The object of criticism—popular culture, the middle class—displaces from the center an entire political-economic-cultural system—late capitalism, consumer capitalism—with its visible faces. Simpson is the example of the naive and decadent worker with an intelligent daughter, an eternal promise of future change, and an exploitative capitalist boss, clearly a bad guy. Even the boss, ambitious, corrupt, and a millionaire, is a middle manager—one of the cats—who concentrates all the evil of the system he represents. The system, like the good king, washes its hands and justifies any pain, injustice, mediocre reality, or oppressive reality by the existence of bad middle managers, by the existence of the cats that play with the mice.

Wednesday, December 24th. Dow Jones: 8,433
New York, New York. 3:15 PM

At three in the afternoon, dusk falls at the foot of the Empire State Building, and the twilight lingers until four. There is a moment when the sunlight has declined too much, and the city lights have not yet turned on, and the streets of the Village and Midtown resemble a languid past and a future of disaster movies. Then the light changes, and the white walker of the traffic light legalizes the pedestrians crossing, paying no attention except to some cars that threaten to run them over. A black limousine cuts diagonally across Fifth Avenue, and an old man with the build of a young man steps out slowly, smoking a cigar. A Sikh with an orange turban at the wheel of a yellow cab zigzags to avoid the playboy and crosses on red. The cold cuts through the hands and the exposed parts of the faces. Despite all her coats, Lupita feels an unbearable cold. She thinks it's the lack of habit, because the people strolling along one of the most expensive streets in the world smile as if they are happy, as if they enjoy such cold. It's the time for Christmas shopping, that must be why. Or maybe it's not why. Manhattan is like this, always happy, always indifferent. So many people, Lupita thinks, so many people and all of them alone. Ernesto, the Uruguayan with the little leather notebook and the Scottish cap, watches her from a Starbucks and writes, "She stops in front of a window where Santa Claus, with mechanical movements, waves with both hands. He's a mechanism. He looks like us." Liz says that Santa Claus, in the Coca-Cola version we know today, was, whether deliberately or unintentionally, the perfect way to de-Christianize Christmas. In a town with such a strong Jewish community and such deeply rooted Christian convictions, there was no better way to disguise such a contradiction, according to which the best allies of Christians are members of a religion that outright denies Jesus as the son of God. They don't even consider him a prophet, like Muslims do. Nothing. Just an impostor with good intentions. Ernesto waves his hand in front of his face and shoos these thoughts away like flies. He sits watching the river of Fifth Avenue. No one touches each other as they pass. It's that space the Anglos put between one person and another. The same space they put between one voice and the next. Latinos touch each other, interrupt each other, and overlap in their discussions. There's a normal meter between two friends talking and a second between one argument and the next. They are colder, crueler, more respectful. In-different. One can't imagine how they look at and seduce each other without risking a harassment lawsuit. One can't imagine how they make love with twenty centime-ters of distance between them. His coffee cup clarifies in green letters that *It's our commitment to doing business in ways that are good to the earth and to each other.* Which means that every time Ernesto drinks a coffee, he contrib-utes to saving the planet and his fellow humans. Ernesto crosses it out. He wonders if in fifty years anyone would be able to understand an old irony. Finally, he concludes: "...with variations in shades in the style of Andy Warhol's Marilyn Monroe." Or is it me who feels so alone? Lupita thinks. Lupita stops in front of a window where Santa Claus, with mechanical movements, sways his hips. He's a mechanism. From his eyes come the *jingle bell, jingle bell*. Ernesto sees a very fat lady pass by, walking with difficulty and sucking on a straw that connects the small mouth of a very wide face and an almost nonexistent neck to a giant plastic cup with some kind of soda. A GAP bag hanging from one arm, the promise of distinction and style re-cently acquired by the gaudy woman who, in reality, is a young woman exhausted by the effort of shopping and walking. Ernesto thinks they should invent a "coffee in-dex." The IC would measure the level of education, which in the United States is almost the same as the economic level, based on the number of coffee shops in a given area. Conversely, the soda index, the IS, would measure the de-gree of lower-class consumers, which in the United States is almost the same as the index of skin color and morbid weight volume. Just go to a *mall*, for example, thought Ernesto, the unbearable Ernesto, said Maricarmen, and verify that the more Black people walking around there, the more sodas and less coffee will be available and con-sumed. Coca-Cola versus Starbucks. Poor against rich, Black against white, educated against unemployed, un-reachable SAT and GRE scores of Princeton against tat-tooed fraternities. In a corner next to a Che Guevara portrait stand, the smoke from a cart reminds Lupita of the sunsets in Guatemala. A man who looks Indian but probably isn't Indian flips pieces of something dark that must be grilled meat, burnt meat. Others eat nearby. Che gazes into eternity from the same Korda photo multiplied sixteen times with variations in shades in the style of Andy Warhol's Marilyn Monroe. In a movie Lupita saw as a child in Guatemala, the men of the future ate human flesh. But it was processed, so no one knew it was recycled human bodies due to the food shortage in the future. Or they knew, but it didn't look like human flesh because it looked like cookies, just as a hamburger doesn't look like a cow with a sad face. Soylent Green, the cookies of the future were called. The chiaroscuro of the city and the tall buildings remind her of that movie. And the men eating green soylent, but of another color, as if it were meat from another animal, grilled, charred, almost burnt but with a rich smell, richer than the hamburgers from *Wendy's* when you're hungry. A small lantern lights up the cart, and two blonde women look, comment as if they were art critics, and take photos. One looks like Madonna and the other is, without a doubt, Nicole Kidman accompanied by Woody Allen. Beautiful women always choose rather homely men. Some honking distracts María, who looks at the women watching the Indian grill master and has to jump to avoid being run over by a huge white limousine. Others do the same. They dodge the limousine and the man who appears behind it, with blood streaming from his nose. His hair is tangled and his feet are bare. María walks away as Nicole Kidman approaches the man with the bleeding nose and asks if it hurts. The man says no, shakes his head, and wipes his drooling mouth with his fist. Nicole touches his hair, but the man continues on his way, smiling, as if he were late for a meeting at Macy's. The horns honk, and the women hurry their elegance, almost indifferently. María looks at them and admires them, but a man coming toward her, between two impeccably dressed waiters , interrupts that task. The man has a beard and a smile that doesn't laugh. The waiters, surely Wall Street executives, María thinks, step forward. The other, the third one with the beard, the one with the smile that doesn't laugh, the one with the gaze of Christ who walks like Christ, wears the jacket of an old suit and from the waist down is almost naked, and you can see he hasn't bathed in months. The good thing about New York, says Carlos, is that you don't have to worry about your belongings. When I arrived from Colombia, I didn't dare go out on the street with my Rolex, and Jaime told me something that I later understood was true: look, here no one cares what you're wearing. Actually, no one cares about anything. And Mary thought that no one cares about anything except themselves. But Mary took a step and pushed away the memory of Carlos, who threatened to overwhelm her with his unbearable chatter about high fashion and his job at *GAP* and his Andy Warhol look through black-framed glasses. She followed the man who looked like Christ for a few meters, and perhaps that's why he had interested Nicole Kidman so much, and she saw him slowly pass by a stand where sixteen images of the Virgin with variations like Warhol's Marilyns were for sale at ten dollars each and fifteen for the painting of the sixteen images of the crucified Jesus with different tones and shades like in a Warhol painting. He crossed the street with the green light but parted the sea of people like Moses in the Red Sea and repeated the same steps to the Bank of America lobby. He waited for someone to come out and entered as if it were his home. The lobby was excessively lit, and the letters in blue and red were so strong that they tinted the cement sidewalk. The man climbed onto a narrow table used for signing checks and deposit slips and lay down to sleep. His bare feet looked like the hard feet of a mannequin. Soon after, a man in a black suit and an executive briefcase entered, wearing a soft but exquisite fruity perfume like the ones managers at the *New York Times* wear.

Friday, December 26. Dow Jones: 8,510
Atlanta, Georgia. 4:15 PM

I was waiting for María José when suddenly I felt a kind of muffled tide that left me stunned. Then I realized it was applause. A woman like Marilyn Monroe was carrying a small flag high up and leading the soldiers returning from the war. They say there's always a war in this country. A permanent war for democracy and freedom. I had seen them on TV, and suddenly seeing them there, live and in person, impressed me. People stopped what they were doing, left their hamburgers on the tables, their newspapers on the chairs, their suitcases on the floor, and started applauding. Some shouted *thank you, thank you! welcome back!* and all that. I didn't know what to do, I didn't want to be seen not applauding, so I started clapping too. Everyone was applauding except for one guy with glasses who was reading the newspaper, unmoving, as if the world around him didn't exist. Then a black woman with blonde hair, who was with two little kids who looked like angels with their golden curls, approached the guy with the newspaper and started clapping louder, almost in his ears, but the guy didn't even flinch and kept reading as if the world didn't exist. And

the woman leading the soldiers in khaki uniforms kept
turning around and around, like on a carousel or at a rural
fair where they parade the champions, round and round,
with the little soldiers behind her, their faces like children's, proud of their completed mission. Then the wave
of applause seemed to renew itself, and we all clapped
more and more loudly, I had goosebumps, honestly, because you have to be there to experience it. To be there,
not like the guy with glasses who wasn't there but somewhere else, and it seemed like a Hispanic woman behind
me said that there were people who could read the newspaper in peace thanks to the heroes who went to defend
us and didn't even have the decency to show a little gratitude. I turned around and nodded, and then another person joined in and said "communist, communist" twice. At
that moment, I felt a lot of anger toward people like that
guy with glasses but also a lot of pride for a country that
allowed wayward elements like him not to applaud and
not be arrested for it. Why lock them up? Nino said to me
when I told him, "so they can turn them into martyrs or
heroes later? It's better to leave them free, like that, until

one day we've had enough of all those bad elements and take serious measures.

Nino always has the right words.

Saturday, December 27. Dow Jones: 8,510
Bonita Springs, Florida. 9:10 AM

Dear Susana. I'm sending you a summary, almost a formula, of your first theoretical sketches on *doubling*. From what I gather from your notes, in the first instance, the *doubling-transfer* works within the limited circle of its creation, but in a second instance, it achieves success in society by functioning within it, like nesting boxes, like Russian dolls.

First, the author A (like the creators of Superman) creates a character P that resembles him, like Clark Kent, who in turn represents a social group. Within the framework of fiction, this character doubles into the superhero SH. That is:

$$[A] \rightarrow [P \rightarrow SH]; A = SH$$

In a mythical-ideological space, the doubling occurs as follows: The reader L —who is also a collective reader, Lc, from the moment their reading is not critical but conditioned by the pre-defined mythical-social framework, not only by the series of comics but by popular culture in general— has two levels:

1) intellectual level (where the hegemonic discourse is rationalized and justified) and

2) sensitive level (where fiction materializes in the real world).

The reader L is constructed by fiction, by the collective myth:

$$[L] \leftarrow [P \leftarrow SH]; SH = L$$

Thus, the *doubling-transfer* in a circular manner, since the author, the supposed "creator" of the myth, of the fiction, is none other than a particular reader, perhaps a reader with a special imagination, a specialized and professionalized reader. That is, $A = Lc$.

In Superman, for example, we can see these two levels through the ambiguous dissatisfaction and sense of social injustice of the Great Depression of the 1930s, which is resolved with a confirmation of the established order through a fictional conflict between good and evil that will be resolved by the muscular strength of the superhero, which is the energy derived from the reader's dissatisfaction. According to the early Superman stories, ironically, the superhero of the capitalist world fights for the social justice of workers, against the exploitative boss. But he resolves the conflict by repairing the order, concealing the social structure under the biblical mantle of good versus evil.

As we can see, every neo-mythic story of comics, TV series, or adventure literature has at least two stages. 1) *A basic, quite simple narrative that expresses the myth and establishes the character*. This story is often remembered in several fragments until it becomes ingrained in popular memory and eventually becomes unnecessary. In comics and TV series, it is the introductory narrative. As in mythical narration, third-person narration predominates, "explaining" the phenomenon in a simple way. 2) *The various particular stories*. Normally, these stories are extremely simplified, sometimes addressing and resolving childish problems. They are entirely secondary stories, but they serve to expose and permanently remind us of the original myth and the supernatural characteristics of the hero. But the hero is not constructed by these stories but rather the opposite: it is the already defined hero, the myth, that gives meaning and significance to each story.

Below, I'll send you a diagram that could synthesize this idea. Beware of the Franciscan cold. Hugs,

Ernesto.

Sunday, December 28. Dow Jones: 8,510

Quemado, New Mexico. 3:20 AM

When he found out he had been chosen to go to war, his heart leapt into his throat.

He would soon turn nineteen. He had prepared his whole life, his short life, for that moment. At one point, he feared the war would find him too old, but the news and events of the past few months had gradually left him with the certainty that his time had come.

It wasn't a surprise, but he couldn't avoid the emotions that brought him to his knees, bent over the ground, crying with joy. He ran his hand over his chest, where years ago he had tattooed the name of God, and felt that he was alive. The hour, his most glorious hour, had arrived. He knew he might die soon, but he would do so for his people and for his faith.

His mother cried after him, when she was alone in the kitchen, but she was consoled by the pride of having a brave son, free from the vain rebellions typical of other young people who didn't share their values. She remembered the toys he loved most, the words he repeated most as a child, his childhood dreams of flying to the moon in a ball of fire, his impossible questions: "Why does it rain? Why does the sun rise?" And the easier ones: "Where do people go when they die? Why are we born if we have to die?" Nothing in her routine changed. The kitchen, feigning joy, and hiding her true emotions were her mission on earth. Thinking otherwise would only increase the pain of the inevitable.

The young soldier remembered his first spiritual guide revealing to him the passion and sweetness of eternal truth, which had so often shielded him from madness. On the contrary, he had learned that fear was, at its core, the source of all strength and the deepest path to true faith. Those who do not fear do not believe.

He had learned that death does not exist for those who have lived a fruitful life. Death does not exist for those who have served their nation and fallen as heroes fighting for the values of their ancestors. Hell, oblivion, nothingness were reserved for those who believed in nothing. To some extent and for the same reason, he respected and valued all the enemies who would die on the battlefield.

Heaven did not await them, but they would surely be spared the hell that awaits the cynical and the unbelievers. Because even the enemies were necessary to fulfill a destiny, and nothing happened without God's approval.

In combat, he eliminated a hundred enemies. He didn't remember any particular face. He had hardly been able to see any clearly. But he did remember the taste of fear in his saliva and the smell of blood and dust that surrounded him and his comrades one night, many of whom never returned. He did remember that in the face of the vertigo of fear, it was enough for him to repeat three times the prayers he had learned from his first pastor to regain his courage and rise with a fury strong enough to destroy ten men with a single shot.

God gave strength to the warrior and victory to his people. The danger of false idols and barbaric customs had passed, at least until the next trial. For years, the children listened to the hero with infinite admiration. The people honored him until a moderate period of peace arrived, and the hero fell into oblivion and poverty.

However, he knew the world was not a safe place, and soon God's nation would be threatened again, because that's how it had always been, and always, not without blood and pain, the truth had prevailed.

The unusual truce lasted twenty long years. Twenty years of peace and almost twenty of irresponsible joy. Until the skies were once again shaken by terrible explosions and filled with fire.

The old hero marched to war at nearly forty years old, knowing that this time he would not return. This time, he would not receive the fleeting glory of his compatriots, the short-lived fruits of the earth, but the eternal glory of Huitzilopochtli, the most powerful of all gods, the eternal one who had proven for thousands of years that everything else is false and perishable. Everything changes and is destroyed every fifty-two years. Except Huitzilopochtli and the eternal gods of the eternal Aztec empire, he realized without being able to wake up.

Tuesday, December 30. Dow Jones: 8,483
Palo Alto, California. 10:05 AM
Almost a year ago, Lucía had received a check from the federal government for nearly a thousand dollars in her mailbox. To avoid a worse crisis, the government was asking for help in spending money. Willing to cooperate,

Lucía cashed it *cash* but then forgot it in the glove compartment.

—*Consumers of this world, unite* —said the boring Ernesto—. This is how we sustain industries in Asia and Latin America. Once again, the poor and hungry of the world have new reasons to be grateful for the waste we produce here.

Lucía told him that if he had nothing more to inform her about the bad state of the world, then good afternoon, he could leave because there was a line of cars waiting behind her.

In the café at the *Borders* bookstore, he ran into Ricardo Menéndez. The boss was one of those who defended the American custom of buying and throwing away without need, as the only way to generate jobs in the world. Ernesto said that progress based on this excessive consumption didn't sit well with his internal logic. That time, Menéndez retorted that if it weren't for all that is thrown away and wasted in the United States, there wouldn't be so many industries in Africa and Latin America, nor would socialist countries like Venezuela sell so much oil at such high prices, nor would employers like him give jobs to intellectuals like Ernesto so they could have free time to speak ill of the system and well of his wife.

—What do you mean?

—Lucía told me you had complimented her.

—What compliment? We were talking about how cold and distant overly beautiful women in this country are, and that she was one of them. She asked if I was referring to her physical appearance, and I couldn't deny it. Honesty obliges. You don't see many women like that coming out of church.

—I know. That's why I married her. But don't think it bothers me. On the contrary, people recognizing what I have is a sign of rationality.

—For you, she must be a war trophy.

—To each their own. Beauty excites me, and it excites me even more when others covet it. Of course, they'd better not touch a hair on her head, or they'll wake up with a bullet in their skull. Look, kid, as an old man, I know women want men to treat them with respect and dignity. People from high academia who would never look a girl directly in the eye so as not to intimidate her, not to invade her personal space. People who are careful with language and manners, who would never utter a sexist or racist phrase. People who would never let slip a compliment or a gallantry because, to them, women are neutral beings, asexual, colleagues, respectable friends. Then those same women fall in love with romantic men, young or rejuvenated charmers who, to win them over, first boost their self-esteem, which is what women value most. Romantics who bring them flowers and tell them in verse that their smile is like the sea breeze. They fall in love and even get married. In the end, after all these silly things pass, the bored housewives, the proper feminist professionals, desire a macho who humiliates them in bed. Only then do they recover their forgotten orgasmic capacities, desiring everything their education and good morals abhor...

—Let's get to the point. I don't covet her. I just recognize that the woman is excessively beautiful, and she knows it. But I wouldn't dream of having her as a wife. God forbid. At most, I'd tolerate her as a lover.

—*Yep*! But for that, besides the primitive conditions I mentioned, you need to have the means. You get me?

—And I don't fall into your group of compulsive consumers. Two coffees a day don't help the economy much.

—Stop kidding around, Ernesto. I'd rather you compliment Lucía than listen to your nonsense. If it weren't for all those desperate ladies coming out of the *malls* loaded with bags of clothes and other nonsense, thinking they took advantage of an excellent sale, our fabric business would be over.

—Always the same. We're so used to being lied to that it bothers us when it's not true. Lie to me always, as long as it's done sweetly.

—Of course, man, it's like sex. Without fantasy, there's no pleasure. You know what that is?

—But how is it possible to keep all that fantasy alive for so long? Do you remember that health insurance company that kept repeating *"Your health is our passion"*? Maybe because this slogan wasn't entirely believable, to reposition this contradiction, the commercials now include a first clause, more honest, so you swallow the second one with jam. True dialectical capsules: *"Your health is our business, but it's also our passion"*. Meanwhile, for a person to get health insurance, they must first prove they're not sick. So much passion, but not that much. It's logical, from the market's perspective: if insurance companies insured sick people, they'd lose money. And what's the goal of a company that sells health rights?

—Health —answered Ricardo with a smile, knowing Ernesto's ideological quirks.

—Yes, the company's health. The insurer ensures the insured doesn't need insurance before selling it to them. If a health insurance company suspects the applicant might get sick in the coming years, they'll deny the application.

—It's their right to protect their profits.

—If you still want to buy health insurance, you'll have to go to a clinic and spend your savings so a doctor can assure the insurer that you're perfectly healthy. If you manage to do that, you'll get first-class service: the best medicine with the best technology; and if you're hospitalized, you'll have the best menu in the most spacious and comfortable rooms in the world.

—Tell me about it.

—Because that's good service. If you can't, better declare yourself indigent, because the State has good programs for these cases. But remember, you must be either a person of means or indigent, that's the business. *"It's not about the money but buying with your heart"; "Your health is our business, but it's also our passion".*

—You should write a novel from the perspective of an unreliable narrator —Ricardo joked—, that is, reality seen through that fabric where "I love you" means "feel around to see where I stabbed you."

—How are we going to fix that? —José asked worriedly. Lucía knew José didn't have insurance and that if he had reported the accident to the police, they would have arrested him.

—How do you know I don't have insurance, ma'am?

—Because you don't have a driver's license either, José. You're illegal.

—I work for your husband. Don't forget that. If I fall, I...

—I know, José. Don't get nervous. Besides, I already told you it was my fault. I braked too suddenly. You didn't have time. I already explained. Finish your soda and relax. Do you have kids?

—Yes, ma'am. Two, a girl of three and a little boy of four months.

—*Nice.* You must be a very good father.

—Yes, ma'am.

—Don't call me ma'am, please.

Now, if the logic of profit isn't bad even for a socialist living in a capitalist world, why hide it? *"It's not about the value of the gift but that it's given from the heart"*. Sic, *Best Buy*. Perhaps because one can only have blind faith in what is unseen. Our entire culture is based on masks, almost all of them narrative. In the same way, the secular world of capitalism masks itself with the religious narrative that dominates societies like the United States. Like the height of irony, putting an invocation to God on the currency that rules the world and for which so many millions are killed every day. By the way, what's the exchange rate today?

—Some people like to make themselves heard —Lupe complained in a low voice, worried about Maiquito's sleep.

The indiscreet cries of pleasure and the bed's dance on the ceiling came down from room 211 of the *Super 8*. Lupe turned up the TV volume a bit to mask Lucía's mistake.

A young woman from *Best Buy* explained in Spanglish and with bright colors that she had recently helped two children who wanted to give their mother a gift and only had a few coins. She helped them get a modest music disc so the children would have something to give. At the end, the young woman concluded with a moral in the style of the *Exemplos* of Count Lucanor in the 14th century: *"It's not about the value of the gift but that it's given from the heart"*. In another almost simultaneous commercial, Wal*Mart advised consumers to save money in times of economic crisis. And to save, they should go consume at Wal*Mart.

Then, as you know, you have to put up with Ernesto annoying everyone with his little notes from *Starbucks*, and now it seems he's also writing in *Chili's*, another eccentricity of intellectuals, those little notes that the subcontinent's tabloids publish as if they were essays that will save the human species.

The primary sense and goal of the company and the commercial—the economic benefits produced by the sale, large or modest—is hidden behind a narrative that appeals to emotion and a traditional, politically correct discourse. The explicit "it's not about the monetary value but the emotional value" replaces the true meaning of the narrative, which is the implicit opposite: "we don't care about love, but that the children bought, consumed, and behind them and in their own future lies the continuity of these profits." Now, if the logic of profit isn't bad even for a socialist living in a capitalist world, why hide it?

That little notebook with leather covers that absorbs all his frustrations as a part-time writer. I just ask Ernesto to leave me alone, that if he doesn't like how things are, he should go to Cochinchina. We don't need people here to ruin the party. You should fire him. But it seems you don't care that he flirted with me. I told him to leave of his own accord, since the boss doesn't budge. And he, again, *sour* as he is, tells me it wouldn't be a bad idea, that if everyone went home, the world would be free of invasions more important than his. He thinks I didn't realize he was referring to the troops in Iraq. You have to be consistent, I say.

But why did Lucía have to go to a grimy *Super 8*, those motels run by Indians where yellow-bearded, red-skinned truckers, passing illegals, long-haired students, and unscrupulous lovers stay? To relive her adolescence, she thought, because youth wasn't eternal, and with it went the charms, the fantasies. The insufferable Ernesto was right about one thing; youth makes any woman beautiful. It had been like a subtle warning, like a damn revenge, the perfect thorn with the acidic style of his indelible signature.

A silent tremor ended with her eyes and mouth wide open. For a moment, José was scared.

—Are you okay, ma'am?

Wednesday, December 31. Dow Jones: 8,499
Carpinteria, California. 8:05 AM

Sitting on the toilet, Ernesto wondered why the act of defecating wasn't more clearly expressed in cultures, in civilizations like the Egyptian, the Christian, or the Aztec, where life cycles had so much importance. At least as a central symbol of the underworld, in the Hades of the ancient Greeks, in the She'ôl of the Hebrews, in Hell among Christians. Was it more elegant to condemn a murderer, a rapist, a homosexual, or an atheist to eternal fire than to send them to shit?

Classical psychoanalysis had dealt with these taboos when it divided societies into oral and anal. Ernesto remembered a book he had really liked in early adolescence, a gift from Emilio, the taxi driver and reader uncle from Buenos Aires, *The Fear of Freedom*, by Erich Fromm. The anal character was the product of the pleasure of retention, the foundation of capitalism, and if he remembered correctly, Jean-Paul Sartre himself had synthesized it in the formula *gold = excrement*. Or had it been him in one of those ironic books that two hundred unsuspecting readers bought each year? As if the anus and the mouth could explain societies and sex, ultimately explaining personal traumas. But capitalism is not what it used to be—or it must be said that it is no longer defined by its anal character but by its oral character, not by the retention of savings but by the pleasure of consumption—nor in either case does it lack sexual implications, since sex is the ultimate element, the irreducible particle of psychoanalytic theory, just as chance is to Darwinism.

But even setting aside this theory, why didn't excrement and defecation have their counterpart in cultures throughout history, like the repression of sex and the fear of death? Or is it that we don't see what is present everywhere? For the indigenous peoples of America, gold was the curse, death opposed to blood, the fuel of life. By transitive property, it should be deduced, then, that if *gold = excrement* and *excrement = death*, $\rightarrow$ *gold = death*. Which forms a rigid congruence of two seemingly disconnected theories.

But who knows if all of this isn't expressed in a more subliminal way. The biblical prohibition against eating leavened bread has no rational justification. Unless the legislators of the time wanted to avoid gas on sacred dates and in sacred places. If menstruation was an impurity in women that imposed on a pure man the prevention of touching her during those times, what wouldn't a flatulence be on a sacred day? Researchers have taken the curious task of counting the manifestation of these natural phenomena and have established that, at least in the West, each individual relieves themselves fifteen times a day. Ernesto was surprised by the number, but respectful of science, he accepted it without bothering to verify the fact. How would a pure man avoid these fifteen flatulences on a sacred day in a sacred place where, for some reason, incense or ox meat was burned to please God? By avoiding this and that food, which is the only thing written in the law.

The lavender soap—that scent loved by the ancient Egyptians, he thought—brought him back to the world of the living.

Wednesday, December 31. Dow Jones: 8,638
Philadelphia, Pennsylvania. 2:00 PM

People began to gather early at the Hispano Mercado, right at two in the afternoon, the time marked on the tickets. María José thought that at that time they would raffle the car, but first they handed out boxes with clothes, pans, and beer. The first chosen by chance weren't very happy, and the rest endured an hour on their feet until finally a curly-haired woman announced that now they were going for the car.

Fatigue gave way to a slight expectation, almost the desire for it to be over once and for all. Next to the curly-haired woman stood the owner, a Chinese man who responded with gestures to the woman's Spanglish questions.

—Attention, ladies and gentlemen. We are about to begin the car raffle.

(Cheering, whistles, suppressed laughter, suppressed shouts, always suppressed).

—Atteeeention! —shouted another employee, with a solid belly, a goatee, and a construction-site voice that dreams of being a baritone— Attention, if you don't stay quiet, we won't raffle the car!

—We're going to draw three names, the first one gets the car— says the curly-haired woman and gestures to the owner. María interprets that the woman is going to chop onions and the Chinese man is going to fry them.

—No —corrects the woman— we're going to draw ten numbers and put them in this hat. Then we'll shuffle it. We'll draw one number, and that's the winner, agreed?

(Cheering, whistles, suppressed laughter, shouts of approval.)

The woman puts ten tickets in a hat, and the Chinese man snatches it from her hand. The woman struggles for a moment, but a slap on her hand convinces her to do what the owner wants, though no one knows exactly what that is. The woman tries to explain, but the Chinese man throws the tickets into the urn where they were. He signals to a young woman who was there, and she approaches, reaches into the urn, smiles at the crowd, and hands a name to the Chinese man. The Chinese man lifts the ticket and gives it to the bearded employee to read the name.

—*José María Telechea!*

—Is José María Telechea here? José María Telechea, once, José María Telechea, twice...

—Here he is, here's José María Telechea.

José María Telechea raises his hand and hurries to push through the crowd of people congratulating him.

—Congratulations, Mr. José María Telechea, you have won the car. Congratulations, you have won the car...

—No, no, no, no, —the Chinese man quickly says with big gestures. He explains something with his hands and says:

—No win, no winner yet, no yet...

Then the curly-haired woman and the employee argue with the owner, and finally the woman explains with a smile:

—Actually, we're drawing ten numbers. The first nine are not winners. The winner is the last one. Do you agree?

—Yes! —the crowd shouts.

—Guadalupe Machado? Guadalupe Machado? Where is Guadalupe Machado?

Guadalupe Machado raises her hand, confused. She doesn't know whether to smile.

—There's Guadalupe Machado. Guadalupe Machado is not the winner. We have to draw eight more numbers.

Cheers of joy. Some laugh, others protest.

Wednesday, December 31. Dow Jones: 8,668
Laurel, Montana. 5:05 PM

It's been a number of years since I've been on this side. I came after Salinas. My town didn't exist on the map until he arrived. We made a living by sewing shirts and pants. In the town, everyone had one of those little machines that made the stitches, and we lived well. Until they said the president was going to pass through Guanajuato, and someone had the bright idea of inviting him to see the town's progress. And when Salinas saw that we were doing well, he ordered them to tax us. Who would've thought of shouting about how well we were doing with the clothing business? They put the town on the map, alright. They started punishing the poor people with taxes, and little by little, it all went downhill. And as if that weren't enough, since they saw the business wasn't bad, they brought Chinese workers to the town. The workshops filled up with Chinese workers. So, if something cost two hundred pesos, the Chinese would do it for fifty. Later, I set up a little taco and soda stand, and the family came down on me, saying I had to pay a thousand pesos for protection. What protection? I asked them. It's not a bribe, you see. It's a vaccine. They charge the vaccine, as the Colombians say. Do you know what the family is? Tomorrow, they told me. Tomorrow, the thousand pesos, or we'll leave you full of holes. I laughed until a neighbor told me that someone had already died like that, that I'd better pay them. And where was I supposed to get it if I was just starting out? All that finished off the work that was left in the town, and I had to leave. And even though I miss it, I still can't get used to it. Look, it's been so long since I came to this side to pick fruit, and I still can't get used to it. I can't even speak English beyond what's necessary for the job.

Wednesday, December 31. Dow Jones: 8,668
El Reno, Oklahoma. 6:15 PM

—Ernesto, someday you'll have to admit that in Latin America, leftist politics is the continuation of literature by other means.

—Well, mate. Although not all of it, I don't deny you have a point. You see, even right-wing people like you are capable of producing interesting ideas.

—It's just that reality is almost never interesting. You poets don't want to accept it, and that's why you produce more interesting ideas than are possible or necessary.

Many interesting ideas, but very few have anything to do with reality.

—The good thing about reality is that it can always be seen from a different point of view. Which doesn't mean there isn't a concrete reality but precisely the opposite. We are a poetic continent. That's our reality, if you'll allow it. Or we were. For some reason, the poor countries of the Caribbean top the annual list of the happiest countries in the world. Amid so much pain and so many injustices, if you're not a poet, you're done for.

—But that doesn't stop them from jumping into the water to chase the American dream.

—Evidently, not everyone. In cases like yours, there's no mystery. In other cases, sometimes it's hunger and other times the spirit of adventure that drives the Latino. It's not the adventure of a pirate; it's the adventure of Don Quixote in the belly of the beast, as Martí said. Che, who called his adventure Rocinante, seriously considered getting a scholarship in the United States or France.

—Now I understand why the United States and France offer such good scholarships to study Marxism in their universities. Marxist socialism was born under the name of scientific socialism and drew its greatest inspiration from Latin American art. But apparently, art is always more dangerous.

—Everyone draws inspiration from what they can.

—What was Che if not a radical poet? He wasn't a poet who dedicated himself to something else. He was a poet who didn't dedicate himself to writing poems. A poet who dedicated himself to making poetry, even if his verses gave more than one person a headache. He grew up and died with a book by Pablo Neruda. His written poems weren't that good. He was better at theorizing, writing in prose, poetizing reality, realizing poetry. He could have become one of the writers of the Latin American boom if he hadn't taken it all so seriously. He took the opposite path of Cervantes. The same path as Don Quixote, from letters to arms. And later, when he had some success, he couldn't settle for reality. That idea of a world without money, without reluctant work, without selfishness... A New Man. Very beautiful. And his speeches, my God, that was also pure poetry. Even Salvador Allende had copied his tone, which in turn was an improved version of those wave-like exclamations of the Pacific that Pablo Neruda recited. It's the José Martí complex, another poet, like all the guerrillas. Even a military man like Chávez is obsessed with literature, which says a lot. That habit of gifting books to their enemies paints the leftists from head to toe. Or reciting poems in the middle of those endless, kilometer-long speeches, like Fidel's, reminiscent of *One Hundred Years of Solitude*. Although, to tell the truth, the only one who made no sense for poetry was Fidel. But he was another master of prose. Another man of literature, but with a certain sense of reality. That's why he could keep going.

—I see where you're going, Ricardito. Now, if you're a poet and you declare that the square of the hypotenuse is equal to the sum of the squares of the legs, that doesn't make it any less true. At least in Euclidean space, that is, human space.

Wednesday, December 31. Dow Jones: 8,668
Valparaiso, Indiana. 8:00 PM
Finally, Ernesto had decided to go to the car raffle at the *regional farmers' market*. The *Hispano Mercado*, as it was painted in giant letters, was a little Central America with a few Chinese neighbors and organized like a labyrinthine *bazaar* from the Arab world. As soon as you enter that world, you forget the perfection of the *malls* and American supermarkets and step into a time outside of time.

There's no smell of *barbeques* or hamburgers or fried chicken. They are smells from the south, from the tropics. The faces too, except for a few curious Yankees. In some stalls, mountains of fresh tomatoes at 45 cents a pound, kiwis, bananas, mangoes, and papayas are piled up. In other corners of the labyrinth, dried fruits like in old Jerusalem, a Turkish bazaar full of carpets and colorful fabrics, a barbershop like the one in Ernesto's town back in Nicaragua, with old chairs and armchairs, with clients telling stories of fertile women and scarce crops. In a stall of ordinary paintings, landscapes with blue waterfalls, little Swiss houses with children playing in the meadow, a blond Jesus with all the variations of the same pose looking with his sweet blue eyes at the Virgin of Guadalupe, looking sad with his black eyes in his vaginal halo.

In one corner, Ernesto found a small restaurant that reminded him, with its smells, its people, and its sand-colored walls and fake wooden port windows, of Alejandro's inn, his uncle from Guatemala. He ordered a tamale and a small jug of apple cider and sat down to remember.

All that he remembered was from the forties. Or the thirties. He couldn't have lived it except in the stories kept at Uncle Alejandro's inn in San Pedro, or at the barbershop of the Tico from Tipitapa, or from the Rivera grand-parents who never stopped telling how hard those years when Sandino was killed, the hated reign of the Somozas that Ernesto now remembered with such nostalgia, with an incomprehensible nostalgia for times gone by that made him forget for a while that any day now he might not be able to pay the bills or the rent, that immigration would be waiting for him on his way home to arrest and deport him to those places in Nicaragua that no longer exist as they do here, in the magical bazaar of the Hispano Mercado, without immigration, without bills due or already overdue, without the remittance waiting, without the death and the widespread pain of the Somozas, with-out the disputes of the Ortegas, the Chamorros, the Ale-máns, with nothing more than that priceless feeling of being outside the world, in a time that has passed, that is already resolved, that does not exist. That sweetly does not exist.

And wanting to prolong that magical moment as long as possible, he ordered another Peruvian pisco. And he kept drinking a few more until he fell asleep leaning on his arm, and a guy with a Mexican accent patted him on the back and asked:

—Brother, what's going on with you? It's really late, we have to close.

Was it then that he realized he had missed the raffle, despite the shouting that he only now remembered, calling out, "Is Mr. Ernesto Lugares present?"

Saturday, January 3. Dow Jones: 9,034
El Cerrito, California. 7:30 PM

The mask, says Susana, is the way to make ultra-visible an element that in reality must be hidden: the double personality of the hero and the reader, the fracture between discourse and action.

In the case of Superman, the mythological hero appears unmasked. It is Clark Kent who masks himself. Superman is the authentic expression of the two: Clark is the myth disguised as an ordinary man, hidden behind glasses that replace the mask of the Gothic hero and a false appearance of cowardice. For the comic, the "true American" is the superman from another planet who hides in the mediocre office worker Clark Kent. For reality, the true American is the repressed Kent who dreams of a superpower that will remedy all the humiliations of the beautiful Lane in the eyes of the true readers, the true

Lanes. The repressed office worker repeatedly saves the beautiful fool who humiliates him insistently. But since this is not true, the office worker must dream of a mask, of a secret hero who pretends to hide.

What is the point of Superman hiding his identity with the mask of Clark Kent when Superman is a legal hero? There is no satisfactory explanation for this question within the comic. Outside of it, this fact means that the miserable Clark, the journalist, the illustrators, the readers of the Depression, that is, the real side of the comic, are not such but a mask of something superior that is not seen, but is suggested to exist. The cowardly Clark is actually Superman, a comic variation of Nietzsche's Superman; the timid and poor illustrators, rejected and humiliated by all women, are actually the genius creators of Superman; the miserable comic readers dissatisfied with their routine and insecure lives are, in reality, secret agents of a world superpower, the power of good, democracy, freedom, and justice.

If dreams express repressed desires in a way that does not offend the moral sensibility of the dreamer, we can say that ideological narrative in popular culture *expresses what it represses and represses what it expresses*: it cannot do so directly, as an analytical discourse, but always in an indirect way: what is expressed cannot be evident for mass consumption, and this concealment of what is expressed is achieved by exalting the opposite: if the system represses the workers' feelings of frustration, it must express these same feelings as a form of consolation and resolution.

This is what appears explicit in the early stories of Superman, that is, in the birth of the capitalist Superman, according to Susana.

Monday, January 5. Dow Jones: 9,027
Rio Rancho, New Mexico. 8:30 AM
Guadalupe was plucking the feathers of the chickens that were passing by on the conveyor belt at the poultry plant. Anita said that in Spain they called a penis "polla." Luisa didn't understand how the penis had a female name, and Raquel grabbed a plucked chicken by the neck and showed that it looked just like a dying penis. But why female? Then Laurita, who is Uruguayan, but spends her time reading things about Mexicans, said that Quetzalcoatl had created humanity by dripping blood from his penis, and she lifted a freshly slaughtered chicken to illustrate her point, the silly girl said.

That time, says Guadalupe, I was half an hour late because I stopped by the *Dollar* store to buy a couple of things. Jackson watched me, but he couldn't say much because it was the first time in months. Raquel and Lupita were discussing the prices of vegetables at the farmers' market when suddenly there was a jolt. It wasn't noise. It was one of those impacts you feel inside, as if you suddenly fell off a cliff without actually falling. Everyone looked around until they saw that the silent wave was coming from the entrance of the plant. Lucía was asking what was happening.

First, a man in a black overcoat was talking to Jackson, who was shaking his head. Then another man, just like the first, entered, and the three of them went into Jackson's office. There had been an anonymous complaint. Then María, who had been there longer than the others, took off her gloves and left her station. Paca followed her, and after a nervous hesitation, Guadalupe did too. But they didn't have time to escape because a hundred or a hundred and fifty other workers had already beaten them to it, and two police officers locked the exit door.

They took us out into the cold and lined us up against the wall. I had an awful urge to go to the bathroom, and the cold was giving me cramps in my bladder. I would have done anything they asked just to let me go to the bathroom, but the answer was always "don't move," which maybe meant they hadn't understood me, said María José. Guadalupe said nothing. She was trembling inside and out.

All I could think about was Maicol, my little one, and if they took me away, I wouldn't be able to give him his morning kiss when I left him with Florita. And Florita, poor girl, what would she do to feed herself and Maicol. I told the police I had two children to take care of, to be kind and let me go, and the others protested that they all had daughters and sons and some also had husbands and homes and would be left with nothing, so I shut up and started crying like a fool.

—*Keep quiet! Don't move!*

Like a fool, because in my case I had a man, a good man like José, who would take care of them.

—*Keep, keep quiet, you're making too much noise!*

Even though José wasn't the father, I knew he would take care of them as best he could. His biggest problem was that in construction, one day he was here, and the next he had to go to another city or state. And when they sent him in the truck with a load, it could be ten days before I saw him. José was a good man.

"Yor aydí," the woman said when it was my turn. And I, who hadn't been paying attention to what the others were doing because I couldn't stop thinking about Maicol and Florita, didn't know what to do, and the policewoman shouted louder, "yor aydí."

—*Your ID* —one of the workers next to her repeated—. She wants you to show her your papers.

I gave her what I had. My ID and the little card Jackson gave me when I started at the plant. The policewoman looked at the card from one side to the other, wrote something on one of those machines they use at Walmart to change car tires, and called someone else.

—You shouldn't have brought the Social —the other one said without looking at her. It's better to be deported than to be caught with a fake number.

—How was I supposed to know? Jackson gave it to me.

—He's a conman —said the Argentine woman who hadn't been checked yet—. He's the worst of them all.

—But I didn't know —Guadalupe insisted.

—You had to know it —the policewoman said while waiting with the radio in her hand.

The others fell silent. The ICE woman had been understanding them from the start. How hadn't they noticed, with that Niurka Marcos face? The problem with Niurka Marcos types is that you never know if they're Latina or American, not even when they open their mouths. They don't have an accent when they speak English because they've been here since they were little, but they understand even the subtlest insults in Spanish. But if you imagine them without the uniform, with their hair not dyed and without the blue contact lenses, you immediately realize they're just like us. That's why they're hired and why they make so much money—they're essential when it comes to hunting illegals. Later, when they take you to a public defender, if they even take you, they say they'll give you one who speaks your native language to protect your rights, and then it turns out the guy can barely tell the difference between grabbing a "polla" in Mexico and grabbing a "polla" in Spain.

The Niurka grabbed me by the arm and pulled me out of the line against the wall. I asked her where she was taking me, and she didn't say anything, as if suddenly she didn't understand.

—I have a fifteen-month-old boy and a ten-year-old girl waiting for me. I'm their only support. The older one takes care of the little one, but if I don't get home in the afternoon, the older one will get very scared. At least let me make a phone call.

Guadalupe takes out her phone from her pocket, and the policewoman snatches it from her.

—Please, miss, I need to call my daughter. She's alone at home.

—That's illegal too —the policewoman finally said and pushed Guadalupe into a white van with barred windows.

When they arrived at the police station, they sorted the workers into different sections. In a spotless room, like Dr. Durham's, a woman who looked like Jennifer López told her to undress after removing all her personal stuff. While Guadalupe searched her pockets, the Jennifer covered her hands with white latex gloves as if she were about to operate on someone or as if she were going to examine her vagina, like the midwife who rushed to attend to her in Houston and stuck her hand into Guadalupe's bloody uterus as if she were unclogging a pipe.

In a gray plastic container, like the ones at the entrance checks of federal buildings and Ernesto says at airports too, Guadalupe placed all her personal belongings. José's watch. A lipstick she used against the cold. The costume jewelry bracelets for Florita. But the Yankees don't know what the Three Kings are. Not even the Jennifer, who must have been another Latina and who labeled the gray container as *personal property*, because for the Yankees, that's sacred. Like the law, because this is a country of laws, unlike Mexico, where Guadalupe had to flee with Florita. Two dollars and some change left over from the five she used to pay for the gifts. The apartment keys along with the keychain-flashlight José gave her. Maiquito was a citizen because, even though the monster Inocencio got her pregnant in Morellos, she gave birth to him in Texas. "My little Yankee sweetheart," José would joke. The crumpled receipt from the *Dollar* store. The purse with the perfume and the feminine pads she had forgotten in the plant locker. More quarters, which Guadalupe didn't know where they came from. And the little red car she bought at the *Dollar* store in People Plaza, because tomorrow was Three Kings' Day, and Maiquito went crazy for the little wheels he called "tiqui-tiqui," just like he called the door "mama" when it opened.

Mama meant *mama* but it also meant *the door is opening.* Now, every time the door opens, *mama* means *she's not here, she's gone, tiqui-tiqui.*

Tuesday, January 6. Dow Jones: 8,954
Arroyo Viejo, California. 8:20 AM

The superhero responds to and serves a dominant force that is, at the same time, visible and hidden, legal and clandestine. Like the CIA and all the secret services that states have created to exercise their legality. The legitimacy of the hidden is granted by the legality of the apparatus it serves. But both the methods and the objectives are dark or have been concealed for greater effectiveness: secrecy is the excuse for a strategy in the name of good. Reality becomes the symbolic space: the general objective, the dominance of an ideology, of a dominant power, is hidden behind the mask of visibility. In the symbolic space, darkness, illegality, and illegitimacy are displaced onto the villains. For the inhabitants of comic books and movies, the superhero acts visibly in favor of the dominant order but hides something the reader knows: the hero's secret (1) is an innocent secret and (2) is necessary for the effectiveness of good, of the visible law, even if it's through muscular methods not foreseen by the system or the legality of due process. For the reader, nothing is hidden, neither the hero's secrets nor the villains' bad intentions. This is true, but only within the framework of fiction, of reading.

However, the purpose of the entire comic is hidden from the reader. The mask is the entertainment and innocence of the cultural product. Reality, on the other hand, is the symbolic space, the dominant ideology, and the hegemonic culture embodied in concrete stories, in popular culture.

Wednesday, January 7. Dow Jones: 8.769
New York, New York. 5:15 PM
I've read in the newspapers that in some part of the world, a hundred children have been killed and many more torn apart in just a few days of bombings. I haven't read it in such harsh words. The press always takes care not to hurt the sensitivity of civilized people like us. But still, I wonder, as I peacefully sip my morning coffee, what kind of human beast could have perpetrated such a deed?

I don't want to think it was just a mistake, another collateral effect, as they always say. I won't think it was the work of smart bombs, because our civilized world doesn't commit barbarities like in other parts of the world and in other times, like in one of those barbaric kingdoms where women dress too much, as in Asia, or too little, as in Africa. On what rights could such crimes be perpetrated? What god could justify so much pain and so much injustice? Because isn't it an injustice, a hundred children crushed and torn apart for Liberty, Civilization, Law, Justice, and the best Reasons? Under what noble arguments could such animal brutality be perpetrated to turn it into pure human savagery?

The governments of the world have demanded a more satisfactory explanation of what happened.

Tuesday, January 20. Dow Jones: 8.105
Lincoln University, 11:55 AM
Consuelo's smiling face filled the CBS screen for five seconds. Below it said *Philadelphia*, but in reality, Consuelo Jackson-Rodriguez was in the Humanities theater at Lincoln University, more than an hour from Philadelphia. Her black, or almost black, face, like Obama's,

followed Sasha's and Barack Obama's as he was about to assume the presidency. The room erupted in cheers. Tears began to stream down her face, dripping onto her hands, which anxiously clutched a cell phone while John Biden smiled with his whole *no problem* face.

Consuelo forgot to call her mother to ask if she had seen her as the world had, witnessing a historic day. The crowd braved the polar cold in Washington, and in Lincoln, the snow shone abundantly under a sunny day. *Yes, we made,* her friends repeated as they hugged each other.

The spectacle of history had momentarily suspended the crisis that loomed like a winter shadow over the entire country.

—But this is the moment of history —said a professor—, and history is the most important thing.

—It's a dream, I'm dreaming —said Consuelo, as she walked without looking where she was going, talking on her pink cell phone.

—*Oh, my dear, unfortunately, I couldn't see you. I was finishing the bathrooms on the second floor. But I can imagine it all, your beautiful face all over the world.*

Until her voice broke, and she had to cough to hide it.

—I never thought this day would come. Can you imagine, Mom? Now they'll finally give you your papers.

—*I hope so, my dear* —murmured her mother, wiping her nose with a tissue.

—Of course, Mom, you won't have to hide anymore.

—*May God hear you, my dear. I'm sure He will* —said Guadalupe, tossing the bloodied tissue into the trash bag.

Again, that sharp pain like a knitting needle piercing her insides. Then an almost pleasurable relief that made her lose her balance. A young man in a hurry came in and started urinating in the urinal next to her. It's the chlorine, Hortensia would say. It's the stress, Ramona would say. This happens to us because we never get a vacation. It's the caffeine. The young man zipped up, quickly washed his hands, and left. It's the lack of relationships, Guada, it can't be like this. The tissue fell to the floor. Guadalupe bent to pick it up, and again, the stabbing pain. It's the cholesterol. It's all in your head. If I don't think about it, it doesn't hurt. But you think about it when it hurts. It's the lack of sleep. It's just laziness that's come with age. It's the caffeine. It's the Raid. It's the cold.

Everything will change soon. Whether she said it just to say it, or just to prolong the illusion, it wasn't noticeable. Mom is always happy, you know.

Wednesday, January 22. Dow Jones: 8.224
Santa Clara, California. 10:45 AM

If there's a country in the world that is almost unanimously associated with materialism, it's the United States. However, Susana says, if we compare this country to any other in Latin America, Asia, or Europe, in none will we find as many churches, and in almost none as many attendees in God's temples on Sundays. Particularly in the South, people don't ask if you believe in God or if you have a church, but rather which church you attend every week. Not owning a car or not having a religion with its corresponding church draws curious glances. No one in the United States is so poor as to not have a car and a religion.

This mask is not strange. Especially in a culture where Calvinist ethics and theology have largely persisted and dominated. According to this way of perceiving God, Jesus, the spokesperson for his father, God, abhorred the accumulation of material goods. But his father, God, demonstrates his preference for his chosen ones by providing them with material wealth.

The need and practice of dedicating five days to financial temples and one day to the weaknesses of the flesh lead to the consequent need and practice of dedicating one day to God. With its corresponding fanaticism, which is nothing more than the result of a masked soul.

Friday, February 6. Dow Jones: 8.280
Boston, Massachusetts. 6:30 PM

The same man with the black-framed glasses and gray beard had been at a lecture given by a soldier at the University days earlier. We know it's the same person because photos don't lie.

We had all gone to the Community College Auditorium to listen to soldier Robert González, who had returned from the war a month ago. Robert González had been recruited without being a citizen, but upon his return, the government rewarded him with citizenship, which was the least they could do for a hero of our community who shows us, once again, that *Yes We Can* is much more than a simple slogan. And I couldn't miss that opportunity to show my middle school kids another example of what I always say, that this century is the century of Hispanics in the United States, that the forty-five million maids, construction workers and soldiers of today will be ninety million professionals, doctors, and generals when they grow up, and that in this century we will see the Gabriel García Márquez and Diego Armando Maradona of the United States.

But something or someone had to ruin it all. Or maybe not, perhaps I'm exaggerating, and the intruder didn't ruin everything if my kids didn't understand the point of the outrageous question this individual threw like a dirty bomb onto the stage where the hero was being honored.

From the beginning, everything had gone well. The students came up to greet him. The College professors, with that eternal style of condescension that consists of being kind to all those of inferior conditions, especially intellectually inferior, as one might assume a soldier or a gardener to be. They approached to shake the thin hands of the warrior returned to his homeland like a Ulysses, to smile at him and make some technical comment about the range of radio waves in the desert or the speed of air moisture liquefaction in a dog's nose. Many people from outside had come, even from the local churches, from all political parties, and even from a Fox TV station. It was the College's big moment to jump onto the state stage or even to have some national presence, if only for a day. But for us, who were truly interested in honoring the hero, it was the first opportunity to see and touch a war hero who made us even prouder because of his Hispanic name.

Everything was perfect, the snacks at the entrance, the flowers for the hero, the speeches by the Dean of Humanities and the president. Only one of the speakers questioned the likely illicit motives of the war, but he excused, as one should, the soldiers who had gone to war in compliance with the law, for their country, in defense of our way of life, of our values.

When soldier Robert González took the floor, he couldn't hide his emotion and tried to conceal his tear-streaked face with the khaki cap that covered his eyes with a crescent of shadow, the result of excessive lighting, poorly calculated or not calculated at all by the organizers, who only got it right with the powerful and moving entrance music that weakened the knees of the most composed. After the emotion, it occurred to me that for some reason music had always preceded the march of armies in times when there were no special effects, or a *Paint it Black* by the Rolling Stones where the helicopter blades are like Napoleon's drums, because music emboldens the hearts of one's own and terrifies the hearts of others.

After an hour of recounting how he had fought alongside so many unforgettable comrades, the final Q&A session with the audience began. By then, he already felt like he was among family, joking, smiling, and thanking everyone, unsure of how to respond to so much praise and gratitude from the audience.

But there was the man with the glasses and the gray beard, asking for the microphone, with that foolish style of someone who pretends to be clueless and doesn't even watch where he's walking. He repeated the previous expressions of gratitude, I think one by one, even echoing the Dean of Humanities' own laudatory words, who was the first to suggest that despite the mistakes of the high command and, above all, the leaders who had decided to wage a war based on apparently flawed information, the honesty of the soldiers who fought for our civilization should be honored with dignity. To conclude, with great respect, he posed his unexpected question in the *lingua franca*:

—How many people did you kill in this war?

A statistical, scientific question, a professor later described it. But clearly biased. The man pretending to be clueless didn't ask whether the soldier had ever killed anyone in his life, but how many. "How many people did you kill in this war?" After all, until not long ago, heroism was measured by the number of infidels killed. Carrying surnames like Matamoros or Killer was a source of pride, and warriors often exaggerated the number of victims of the right hand of God, the liberating arm of the emperor. Later, of course, the cowards hiding behind their countless books and their irresponsible dispossessions began to replace the virtues of conquest with the rights of defense. They infiltrated their poison into our Western civilization, and even we had to change our rhetoric to maintain the practice.

Apparently, there was no reason to be offended or uncomfortable. But the packed audience that afternoon took a deep breath, surely with annoyance. The whispered cry of "*communist*" must have come from the *off-campus* delegation, because that's not the respectful and tolerant style of those who, they say, are accustomed to academic life, even with the most despicable ideas and opinions.

Soldier González finally replied:

—Have you ever been in danger defending your country? What's your name? Where do you live? What do you do for work? What do you do in your free time?

Tuesday, March 3. Dow Jones: 6.726
Gordo, Alabama. 6:33 PM
I'm a Gulf War veteran. This is my enlistment card. These are the boots I wore. The president's letter. The box from my last meal in the desert. I currently weigh 90 pounds. Any help is appreciated. Have a nice day. Drive safely. God bless America and your family.

Thursday, March 5. Dow Jones: 6.598
Amarillo, Texas. 4:35 PM
Ernesto X —as the Texas professor signs his files— confirms his theory about the progressive destruction of language through two phenomena: (1) the overabundance of stimuli where, according to Roland Barthes, language admirably comes to mean nothing, and (2) the progressive grammatical and semantic disarticulation, where, as in narco-street language, articles, pronouns, verbs, etc., begin to be lost in favor of the use of neo-

hieroglyphs. The first is achieved through the stimulation of symbol consumption and the logistical and legitimizing support of a purposefully created intellectual class. The second was achieved, initially and according to the same thesis, through the consumption of Anfora II, the drug designed by the Department of Intelligence for the educated class, which accidentally spread to students and from there to the neighborhoods of Philadelphia.

Apparently, some academics suspected the phenomenon, but their work became incomprehensible to the rest of society, so the same goal was ultimately achieved through an accidentally different path, rendering useless, neutralizing, and isolating one group from the other. In the case of less educated classes, the response to miscommunication is not arrogance but violence, which spreads to the rest of society. Verbal miscommunication also spreads, now not because of the drug Anfora II but because the phenomenon has passed like a virus to the rest of popular culture.

According to the monograph by Dr. Ernesto X, the experiment began in the Hispanic community for two reasons: (1) the phenomenon of losing the mother tongue without fully acquiring the new language was discovered;

(2) a large portion of this community consists of illegal immigrants, that is, human beings who, in reality, do not exist.

The original goal of the Agency was to reverse the process of destruction of Western civilization, but as in previous times, good intentions are not always followed by the best results. But something is something.

Professor Ernesto X is no longer in his position. He had to resign due to an unproven case of racial discrimination or for not following his three-year plan for his *tenure* or for his suspicious research on pornography, according to him, which the Agency detected in time and made known through James, the person in charge of cleaning the offices of the professors at the Humanitas Center, thanks to which this investigation into his hard drives was able to be conducted.

Friday, March 6. Dow Jones: 6.626
Colma, California. 6:15 PM
Mr. Fernando Villa arrived this afternoon, as he had promised. He came alone; he didn't want the opinion of his wife and children to push him into a bad decision. I marked on the map where the Villas and the Fernández

Sotos were, and without saying much, he left for there with his driver.

Mr. Villa's wife was here last week. She came with her dark glasses and her beautiful smile. She asked some strange questions, spent an hour driving around in her car, and then left. She lamented that the dead couldn't move residences when the neighborhood turned bad. She wanted to know if it was possible, and I told her no, that I didn't think it was possible, but she should consult a lawyer. Either she consulted or forgot, but she didn't come back with the idea of moving her family from Camino Real, which, more than a Camino Real, she said, was a highway like any other and full of unknown dead people.

You can't go around moving the deceased, that's why these neighborhoods are called Eternal Home Cemetery, because they're forever, I told her, very respectfully. But she told me that nothing is forever, and maybe she was right, because a large part of Colma's population was displaced by decree from the cemeteries of San Francisco, about a century ago, when land became expensive.

And who knows if one day the big fault line that's just around here doesn't open up and all these little bones end up scattered in the sea. In any case, the residents of

Pacifica are screwed, my son tells me, because they're on the other side of the fault. But I don't trust that only the coastal strip will sink. If the big quake comes, we'll all jump.

My son, who is an economist, always laughs at my fears about the fault. He has a different perspective. He tells me that maybe it wouldn't be so tragic. Just as lands sink, they also rise elsewhere. So if we lose Pacifica and a good slice of the peninsula, we could well gain some island or other, whose real estate value would be incalculable.

Mr. Villa must be of the same opinion. I should introduce him to my son, who always dreamed of working at Google. It's just that Mr. Villa is focused on something else now. For months he's been coming and driving around Colma looking for the ideal spot. What's more ideal than being with his parents, I tell Eusebio, but it's just that Mr. Villa doesn't like the place, or he's not sure about the option, because there's always a better option, especially after the Ayalas built that horrible mausoleum for their daughter Lucy with a crying angel on top of the coffin. It's *kitsch*, he says. They should have painted it gold, he says. Besides, that girl had some habits that scare Mr.

Villa. I don't know, Eusebio doesn't know what habits either, but I think she had tattoos even in places you don't name and shaved her head to show the tattoos she had there. Another one of those crazy girls you see downtown, but she wasn't all bad.

In Colma, we did what we could to present Mr. Villa with all the options available and yet he still can't decide. His only consolation, he says, is that since the options are endless, he'll always have the freedom to choose something better. The problem is that in that process of choosing, death might catch him by surprise. I'm not saying this because Mr. Villa is old, no. He can't be more than sixty. It's just that when you reach that age, I speak from experience, you start thinking about the Grim Reaper, as the Serrat song says. That must be what's happening to Mr. Villa, and that's why he's looking for a place with a good view.

When I found out that the tomb next to Marilyn Monroe's niche in Los Angeles had been sold for over four million dollars, I immediately thought, that's Mr. Villa. Those of us in Colma know that Marilyn's tomb is one of the most popular in her cemetery, so having a name and a place next to hers would boost the sales of any business.

Westwood is tiny compared to Colma, just a little nothing, but you have to admit it has its roster of celebrities. Besides Monroe, there's Dean Martin, Truman Capote, and Farrah Fawcett, the angel who moved there recently. They say that right above Monroe, face down, was a guy named Richard Poncher with a tombstone that read, "To the man who gave us everything and more." But his widow decided to remove him from there, not out of jealousy but because she needed to pay a million dollars for the mortgage on her Beverly Hills home. She put it up for sale on eBay for half a million dollars and bam, bingo. But then it turned out that the Japanese guy who bought it realized he didn't have enough money, and the widow offered it to the bidders who hadn't reached the desperation of the Japanese guy.

I know that Mr. Villa and his wife are heavyweights on eBay. He because he has shares there, and she because she's addicted to shopping. That's what Eusebio told me. But the next day I saw Mr. Villa arrive and I told myself no. But who knows, I say. Who knows if Mr. Villa didn't buy that niche next to Monroe and is still undecided, looking for something in Colma, which is actually the best place, judging by the landscape. Who knows if he's not looking for a second option to later sell the first. Who knows if the niche next to Marilyn wasn't just an investment.

Who knows if it's not actually a gift from Mr. Villa to his wife. Either the one above Marilyn or this one in Colma. After all, the lady really likes ladies. Since she has time, she can always think about other options. And Mr. Villa prefers to see her next to another woman for all eternity rather than endure another affair with one of her gym trainers.

Sunday, March 22. Dow Jones: 7.278
Chicago, Illinois. 9:15 AM

The truth is, Sundays are the worst days. You spend the whole week breaking your back and waiting for the weekend, but except for Saturdays in the park or when it's cold at *Barnes & Noble* reading the *New York Times* for free, I'd rather skip Sunday. I think it reminds us that the old and old friends are far away, not to say they're gone, and you start with *YouTube* searching for "Montevideo" or "Buenos Aires" just to see nonsense from the idiots over there who have nothing better to do than tell how they get drunk on Saturdays and repeat the same things, century after century, as if they were clever tricks. *"Hey, Boniato, you're drunk as a fiddle, tell us how you hooked up with María José and if you like men too. No? You're more wasted than Pico. If you don't say anything, it's because you like men. See, he's not saying anything, tomorrow I'll post it online so your girlfriend knows. Then I'll give her my email in case she needs someone to cool her off."*

Holy crap. That's what technology is for. Like the crazy Gerardo used to say, when he compared the Internet to the sewer system. This is what professors like Ernesto must call the Progress of History. Then you remember there are better things and start searching. *Milonga del pelo largo, Sui Generis* (*...to find one morning, inside my room...*), even *Los Iracundos*, who in Uruguay no one paid attention to and I hated them for being superficial, and I end up listening to them like a fool. *"And today you cry for me, because you're alone, life is like that..."* But the heart remains on the left, and in the end, I think, out of pure anger, I end up with Cafrune again.

> *I know they have an idea of me back home*
> *because I don't kowtow to those in charge,*
> *because despising others' tracks*
> *I know how to open my own path wherever I want.*

My old friends, not to say *ex*friends. When they don't slip in a subtle comment about the reasons I left the homeland, I have to find out from others that So-and-so said this and What's-his-name said that. Or they stop writing, or they disappear. Or they get offended because I spent three days in Montevideo and didn't have time to visit them. After Complaining, Feeling-Offended is the second national sport. They can go to hell, if they want, it shouldn't matter so much to me. Since I left, I couldn't and didn't want to make friends here at the same speed I was losing them back there. Here it is, *The town already has a commissioner*, this is it.

> *Because they haven't seen me lick the yoke*
> *or go around sniffing*
> *to make a buck*
> *and they know full well that I'm tough-mouthed*
> *and no mule's brake can hold me.*

My contradictions. Damn it, I say. Don't we all live in a contradictory world? Why do they blame this poor gaucho who only has a *chiripá*[2] and a bag to cover his ass, who

---

[2] *Chiripá*, gaucho overskirt

didn't invent any of this, who found all of this already here when my poor mother gave birth to me more and more absurd years ago? *Because when I have to sing truths/ I sing them straight, like a man/ even if those truths are full of worms/ where no one thought there'd be any.* They forget to say or don't care to consider that while they, my old comrades, were having business lunches with the sons of the old oligarchy in the name of pragmatism, I was one of the few who said *no* to the cushy job at the Bank handed down by the caudillo. *Because they don't fool me with four lies/, the big shots who come from the people/ to praise devalued currencies/ and make promises they never kept.* And from then on, I started to starve Lucita even more than she already was. Hunger, maybe you can endure it, as my detractors say. *That's why back home they have an idea of me/ because among the ceibos a quebracho stands out/ because they've all been branded/ and they envy me for being free.* What you can't endure is seeing that there's always more country for some than for others, when it's not because of money and last names, it's because the winds of politics blow from the other side. *And what do I care, I'm wild and free...* And aren't the most anti-imperialist countries, like Chávez's Venezuela, which lend their immaculate flags, selling the best part of their oil to the Empire? And the little country too, which now finally claims to be socialist, well, it sells its cows to the same empire. And I'm not going to say that they're feeding the eagles with national meat, with the blood of the ox, nor that those dollars are less holy than the ones I make here, which in this case is just a scratch. So let them stop messing around and leave me alone, I don't have oil wells or feed millions of fat cats so that, well-fed, they can go around invading countries in Asia or conspiring in Latin America.

Damn it, I got worked up again and woke up Lu because I didn't put on my headphones.

And what do I care, I'm wild and free
I don't follow caudillos nor do I cling to laws...

And when I got here, to the heart of the empire, and finally got a job all day and all week and some dollars to live and send to my mother, I couldn't change the Che Guevara record, or I couldn't escape the sea of my nostalgia for that youth when we were happy not because of what we had and surely because of our age we felt free and didn't have a wife or mother to take care of and a glass of wine at the bar on Rincón and Misiones with a Hemingway novel was all we needed. And because you can't hold onto something by keeping it the same, repeating the same thing always, because that's how you lose it, and above all (I should start there) because I lost my job and broke my knuckles knocking on deaf doors, and because the lice were eating me alive in Montevideo and I was already fed up with my own anger at the world, I left, we went to where the dollars are printed and the lights are turned on, and then they also started coming at me with everything because of my contradictions. I didn't leave to get rich and famous, like Hernán Cortés or Aristotle Onassis, because I've always said and still say that the richest isn't the one who has the most but the one who needs the least. And this isn't a phrase to hang on a little frame but what I truly know from my own experience and because I learned it from the gauchos back there and the Buddhists here, though I suspect that I know less and less how to put it into practice, as if the monster's guts have already digested me and who knows where, in what intestine I find myself now and if it's not likely that one day I'll end up coming out the back door, not to say that one day they'll throw me out the ass and then I'll feel liberated or drown in the rest of the shit that the great monster releases over there and rats and mice eat. *I'm richer than those who* *expand their fields...*I was rich when I was young and didn't have so many obligations with their corresponding needs and a Hemingway or Sábato novel was all I needed to feel the world with all my pores. Not like now when the more I have the less I feel things and people and a pencil and a tiny new notebook no longer has the smell it had when I was a child and that was all my capital and an entire existential experience. Now I don't even feel things (let alone people), I use them and they serve me to live, if you can call that living.

and I go through the clear paths of my whim
and I don't need anyone to guide me.

And Lucía tells me, stop singing Cafrune, and I just to contradict her say that they're actually verses by Serafín J. García, another Uruguayan you Argentinians stole, I tell her, just to rile up my dear *porteñita*.[3] And if you think about it, the same author of those gaucho verses, anti-commissar, ended up working as a policeman and even a Francoist-style dictator like Gabriel Terra signed a decree to distribute one of his books in police stations and even

---

[3] *Porteño*, person from a port. *Poreñita*, "young Buenos Aires woman."

promoted the poet to sub-commissar of Santa Clara de Olimar. But to me, the promotion was to get him out of town and bury him in the countryside, since he liked writing about gauchos so much. You have to imagine his wife's face when he got promoted. Like when they published Sor Juana de la Cruz to bury her, one of the most curious and subtle and cruel censorships in history. The perfect kiss of Judas. Shitty world, I say, they don't even let you protest anymore. And what if Serafín was actually a well-off fascist? The truth is I barely remember *Tacuruses* and the dough they gave us at school with *The Adventures of Juan the Fox*. But I don't know more. It's hard to believe, someone who read almost all of Marx and Engels and I think all of Nietzsche and Sartre and doesn't know if Serafín J. García was a fascist or not. And what does it matter? If the soldier-writer was a bootlicker (most likely in his position, though there were notable exceptions like Artigas and maybe Seregni too) his verses aren't to blame. His verses have their own voice or it's the voice of all the others who instead of licking boots have been trampled by those same boots.

Because the pompous guy with a covered kidney
for whom no commissar uses laws

I treat the same as the one who only has
a bag chiripá to cover his ass.

Besides, it was sung by *Los Olimareños* and Jorge Cafrune. And Cafrune was killed by the military for singing, I'd say for being a Marxist gaucho, a mix of Arab poet and Jewish Bolshevik. Look how stupid you have to be. Those military guys weren't satisfied with being fascist murderers, they also had to do everything possible to graduate as idiots by killing a singer to set an example. *Idiots squared*, to the nth power, an indispensable title to become president, governor, or mayor.

But the truth is that without the beard and the Martin Fierro vibe of the Turk Cafrune, these verses wouldn't be the same.

—Sapito, did you have coffee yet?

—No.

—Do you want me to make you some?

—No, I'm drinking mate.

—Did you wake up as a gaucho today? Where did you get yerba?

—There was a little bit left behind the spices.

—It must be like a year old. Isn't it spoiled?

—Bad yerba doesn't die.

—Stop talking nonsense.

Where the hell does that gaucho thing come from that has no place in the world anymore: "I don't cling to laws/ and I go through the clear paths of my whim." Is there a place in the world left without laws? Where did the true solitude go? I mean solitude, which isn't the same as that collective alienation we see every day. The world has already been fenced, closed, and marked with *Do Not Enter. Private Property.*

Good thing I don't feel like becoming a writer, because otherwise I'd have to complicate my week explaining this simple idea that no one will ever understand. Well, at least if I dedicated myself to fiction. They have it easier.

> *Because even though I don't have*
> *a place to drop dead*
> *I'm richer than those*
> *who expand their fields*
> *paying with a stew of dry graves*
> *to the poor peon who leaves his lungs cinching*

And then Lucía comes to the computer and looks up *YouTube* Palito Ortega, who she never liked before and I don't know if she likes now but it's definitely to cut me off.

Happiness, ha, ha, ha, ha.

That your love gave me, ho, ho, ho, ho.

And I, who inside keep going with the tole tole of Facundo Cabral:

I'm not from here, nor from there
I have no age, nor future
and being happy is my color
of identity.

Tuesday, March 31. Dow Jones: 7,608

Altavista, Virginia. 7:15 PM

Honestly, you're cruel, inhuman. If you were going to give the poor guy a few dollars, why did you roll up the window when he approached? What does the sign matter? What does it matter if he participated in that war or any other? After all, he's a human being. Yes, like the others who died. The others of the others, too. There must be a reason why the three *homeless* we've seen so far this year were war veterans. As if that weren't enough, what they do, they come back unhinged, they turn to drugs and go out begging. But what does all that matter, if the guy must have been really hungry. OK, let those who support that garbage feed him. You're inhuman, honestly. You weren't like this before.

Saturday, April 11. Dow Jones: 8,083
La Jolla, California. 9:30 PM

At first, Ricardo was affectionate. He treated me like a queen. He took me to the best stores and let me choose what I liked most. He took photos of me and sent them to his family: Lucy at the beach, Lucy with her friends in Pasadena, Lucy at her friend Ernesto's graduation. Lucy, Lucy, Lucy. He was devoted to me and made me feel like that runway girl I was when I was younger in Los Angeles.

Until little by little he started to change. I don't know if it was his new friends, the flirty colleagues he had at work, or his job itself, especially when the rumors of layoffs started and he knew that if anyone was going to be let go from the technical team, the first one would be him and not that fresh-faced Fisher girl who had the boss hooked like a fish by the mouth; and because he was also the newest in the company.

Around that time, everyone was very nervous because it was said that the automakers were going to go bankrupt, and if Ford or GM or Chrysler went under, Ricardo said, the other two would follow, and the company he worked for would see a drop in software sales. So I would tell him that none of that was a reason for him to stop being affectionate with me. After Obama won, and it wasn't because of Obama but because after the elections it became clear that everything was going to get worse, it was as if suddenly the house had lost its queen. Ricardo's lack of love was justified by the Great Depression that was coming. But for me, there was no other great depression than Ricardo's and his affection. And my own, which was already wearing me down with that situation.

Then we started arguing more and more frequently. I wasn't willing to give up the love Ricardo had shown me at the beginning, and I demanded that he treat me like before. But I got tired of waiting. Once I told him the truth, that he wasn't prepared for the big challenges like a real man, he squeezed the *Starbucks* cup until the coffee spilled and burned his entire hand and stained the magazines on the table. I screamed in shock, and the people next to us turned to look and realized the crazy man I had beside me. They must have understood the situation because we were speaking Spanish, and the macho culture

of Latinos is well known. So every time they glanced sideways, it was like a warning that at any moment they would
take out their phones and report Ricardo as a violent
macho. And to avoid a scandal like that, I would tell him
to calm down, that he was getting more irritable every day
and that he needed professional help. But Ricardo refused
professional help because he mistakenly said that his problems had to be solved in a job he appreciated less every
day, or he preferred to chew on his anger in silence and
who knows what other frustrations he brought home. I
got tired of waiting and went to therapy on my own, and
I managed to rebuild my self-esteem.

But one day he forgot to pay the credit cards, and we
had to pay fines and extra interest, I couldn't take it anymore and told him what he really was, a lazy and worse
lover, to see if he would wake up from his dream. I did it
for his own good, so he would react. Because, by the way,
the truth is that he had never fully satisfied me as a
woman. My self-esteem was at rock bottom. When we
made love, I couldn't reach what a fulfilled woman is capable of reaching with her man, as Rosana told me, and
that was destroying me. At first, I faked pleasures I didn't
feel, but then I realized that wasn't fair, that I was being

treated like a cheap woman who only satisfies the man of the house. One day when we were arguing about another cut in family expenses, I couldn't take it anymore and told him straight out that he had never served as a man in bed, to see if at least he would fulfill his duties as a husband at work.

That's how I spent entire weeks, months, and Rosana and Claudia told me that my life wasn't a life, that it was destroying me as a woman. I also didn't know why I had left Emmanuel Fuentes, who loved me more than Ricardo and who today is the most respected man in Miami in the world of life insurance. And I said no, I said no to Emmanuel Fuentes, because I had fallen in love with Ricardo's blue eyes. How foolish, my God, as if one were to live their whole life off the color of a man's eyes. My psychologist says that it has been studied that, due to a psycho-chemical process, infatuation lasts eleven and a half months. And after that, it's a matter of negotiation for two fulfilled individuals with high self-esteem to stay together. Business, that's what it is, Ricardo would mock, because when it came to irony, he was always a master. Even in that, he was capable of destroying my self-esteem in such subtle ways that I had worked so hard to build.

Once Rosana, who has always been more advanced than me in this, realized something I hadn't noticed before: that I had married Ricardo to have the blue eyes I had always wanted for myself. It was something like the absence of the phallus in women. A genius, Rosana. Emmanuel Fuentes, no, Emmanuel was more of a dark-skinned man, like me, but from the first day we met, he had told me he had a position for me in his company, and I didn't even listen to Rosana when she said the thing with the engineer was just a passing fling. It wasn't a fling, it was infatuation, because it lasted almost twelve months. But if I had listened to Rosana, today I wouldn't be alone and fighting with lawyers over the Boca Raton house that Ricardo still claims belongs to him because he bought it before we got married.

But he lost everything, even the honor of being a man, when that idiot slapped me. When it seemed like everything was going to be fixed, or rather, when he thought he was going to fix everything with a little bouquet of flowers and a Caribbean cruise, it turned out we were going on the yacht of a friend of Ricardo's boss, with another couple I barely knew. And I didn't say it to be mean, but it crossed my mind the good times we had with Emmanuel on his own yacht, which was like saying on our own yacht; because yes, he hadn't formally asked me to marry him, but we already had a very fulfilling relationship. Yes, that was the truth, even if it hurt him, even if it wounded his macho pride, because as Rosana says, men's machismo makes them sick when they know a woman has enjoyed someone else more than them.

So I had to say enough, for my own mental health and self-esteem. I wasn't going to go around begging for a little spot on a yacht when I had my own and when I knew what it was like to feel the fullness of being a woman at sea.

Then the argument turned to Emmanuel, and he started getting furious and yelled at me that I was neither a queen nor a princess, that this is a republican country where women work. To which I asked him if he knew any woman who had earned a yacht by working, because I knew that kind of remark was more typical of a former leftist like him. Emmanuel would have said yes, of course, that many women could have a yacht if they set their minds to it. Even if it wasn't entirely true, at least I'm sure he would have said yes to boost my self-esteem. That says a lot about a man. Working, of course, and I'm sure I could have done it if I hadn't been systematically diminished by Ricardo. But Ricardo wasn't Emmanuel, and in his leftist and macho mind, there was no way a woman could earn a yacht through the honest effort of her work. So he responded by pursing his lips and baring his teeth. In other words, he swallowed his own arguments. He was hurt, because he had also lost in that, and losing to a woman must be the worst thing for a macho like Ricardo.

But if he had lost, I hadn't won. That day with the little gift of the borrowed yacht, Ricardo managed to destroy what little self-esteem I had left and that so many months of therapy had managed to rebuild. I didn't start crying like other times, because over time living with Ricardo taught me that crying was useless. I told him the truth, that as a man he was only good for installing programs, and that's why I had to rely on his employees. The plural was an exaggeration, but I was very hurt, and he didn't believe me. Besides, the point was that I didn't miss Emmanuel's money, that was a real slander, but that Emmanuel did know how to satisfy a woman, because *he had what it took*. And that others, with less money than him, also had what it took, so it wasn't about me being a queen interested in money as he so subtly wanted to make me believe. And again, I almost brought up the issue of José. But I reacted in time and didn't tell him who, how, or where. It would have cost me the Boca Ratón house. Ricardo always carried a digital recorder that looked like a pen, and no one knew. Many times I told him that was illegal, but an oppressor always has their tricks, and he would have used it against me. Something I learned in this country is that intentions don't matter, only words. Everything you say can be used against you. That's why before entering the country, they ask if you want to kill the president. What matters is the statement, not whether you want to or not. The same goes for José and Emmanuel. It doesn't matter if I did it with José or if everything I said about Emmanuel was true. What matters is what was said. And hearing that he was less of a man than Emmanuel and many others with less money than him was the end.

It was when he gave me that slap that made my legs tremble, more from the humiliation as a woman than from the symbolic force of his hand, which couldn't even deliver a proper slap. Then I fell onto the nightstand and knocked the lamp to the floor. Ricardo got scared and threw himself on top of me, begging me to forgive him, saying he hadn't meant to do it, but it was too late. He wasn't concerned that I had fallen onto the nightstand but that I wouldn't report him. But I grabbed the phone and called the police. I called and then said I was sorry, that I hadn't meant to do it. So Ricardo, my little bird, my bunny from the good old days, had no time to do anything but wait locked in the garage for the police to come and arrest him for domestic violence, while he pretended to commit suicide with the car's exhaust, like in the movies.

And if the judge doesn't give him many months in jail, which I doubt because in this country the laws are enforced, at least his next victim will be warned about this violent man's criminal record. And because the law doesn't cover all moral violence, nor is there a judge to punish it, I will make sure other women know and learn from my experience. I'd like my case to be known, which is why I'm thinking of writing a book, so that all women, and maybe some men, why not, who are in the same situation know how to defend themselves and never tolerate any kind of violence.

Still, it won't be a book of denunciation as much as one of help. A book that also teaches forgiveness. Although many people may not understand it, I don't hold a grudge against this man. I know how to forgive, and as a Christian, I am obliged to forgive. As Rosana says, Ricardo is just a victim of the macho culture of our societies, though that doesn't make him innocent or free him from his responsibilities under the law. What matters now is to look forward and work to feel better, to fully realize myself as an individual and as a woman.

I truly feel liberated now. I've been reborn. I've become a woman again, eager to put on makeup to make up for lost time, to hear the compliments of men at parties and in stores, delicate compliments, the kind that lift your self-esteem after the catastrophe of an earthquake like the one I lived through.

Friday, April 17. Dow Jones: 8,131
Opa Locka, Florida. 6:10 PM
Susana stepped into the canal almost an hour before the scheduled time. She had been invited to Lilí's show because they considered her a strange creature. She was introduced as the author of *The Mask*, a book that didn't talk about happiness or how to be happy in eight chapters and an appendix but promised some form of help, though it wasn't yet clear to whom. All that was known was that

the author was a practicing lesbian and a professor at Princeton University.

The stage looked a lot like the one she had found at the *Debate of Ideas*, though much narrower, and almost everyone was dressed in casual sportswear.

She was seated between a specialist in tarot and Chinese astrology and a specialist in exorcism. At one end was the author of *How to Be Happy Despite Your Husband*, and further on was Santiago Petradura, the author of the bestseller *The Power of the Mind*, according to which good things only happen to those who attract positive vibes. It was undoubtedly an exceptional program, as Lilí explained, wrapped in a gray fox fur and accompanied by the famous vedette Reina Narcos.

—"This program by Lilí," introduced the famous host, "is sponsored by *Libertad Stores*, photocopies *El Diverso*, and the *Association for Democracy in the World*, with offices in over fifty countries. We thank them for the opportunity to have a forum today with brilliant guests to debate, discuss, and freely disagree on how to achieve the best happiness for everyone in this world full of violence, misunderstanding, and little faith in our Lord. Today we will not talk about the scandals of the entertainment industry, nor about the latest statements from my friend here present, which all of you have already heard this week… (oh, my God!, this woman is terrible, of the purest Latin essence) but about books, about culture, about all the thought and the beautiful things that our restless people are producing and creating for the benefit of the world.

Reina Narcos, unexpectedly and before speaking in a more measured tone than usual, put on some reading glasses and expanded on the comment from the back cover of *How to Be Happy Despite Your Husband* as an introduction to her own experience of five ex-husbands and six faithful lovers.

—And I discarded all of them when they couldn't please me —she explained with her long nails that adorned her hands, which provoked warm applause from the audience—… because we women have to stand up for ourselves, sir! No to drugs, no to violence!

The only problem came when it was Mrs. Susana Ocampo's turn, as she began to explain her theory of the duality of North American culture as an expression of an imperial complex. The atmosphere began to heat up when Lilí started to refute her guest, supported by the heat of the audience and the disapproving faces of the other four writers. It must have been a production error or perhaps someone thought to boost the ratings with a little scandal.

—This lady, by the way, much younger than me —she could be my daughter—, has read many books but all of the same kind and with the same agenda —said Lilí.

—If by the same kind you mean that they were all critical, radical, well-documented, then you are almost right.

—Professor, you should read books that think differently from all those critics who bite the hand that feeds them. So many books have brainwashed you.

—Which is better than having it dirty, full of media garbage and entertainment propaganda. Now, if you believe and want to make your audience believe that we owe our lives and bread to the rich and powerful who decide which country to invade to protect us and what handouts to give to the poor of this country to keep them content in their urban ghettos and what shows to administer (for free, because that's what democracy is about) to keep them happy and distracted, you can do so. In fact, that's what you've done all your life and that's what you've lived off, right? And no one says that you lick the hand that feeds you. Because in reality, the hands you lick don't feed you, as one might think. Wealth does not *trickle down*, as President Reagan said; it is *sucked up* from above. But don't count on me to feed that fallacy. If I read a lot of the same thing, it's only because I'm interested in reading inconvenient truths. Remember that power (you only honestly administer a tiny fraction of it) is a liar by nature, as it has always specialized in oppressing with the complacency and furious reverence of the oppressed. And although I've read some books on social anesthesia, that's not necessary to maintain a balance. The famous *balance* in favor of the rich. A few critical books, a few radical dissidents, do not mean a real balance. Power and its servants express themselves through other means. Radio, major newspapers, cinema, television. Not to mention the language used on the street. *Liberate* means *oppress*. *Defend* means *invade* some country. Have you noticed that we're always invading some country? Well, it's to liberate it, even if we need to do it by force of fire and imposing governments tailored to our interests. That's why we say that *moderate* is us and all those who follow us and agree with us. The rest are *radicals*. Free radicals.

—If you don't like it, why don't you go live in another country? Why don't you go live in Cuba or Afghanistan?

—To another country? For what? To continue living according to the impositions of the country where I live now? Isn't it enough for you to be almost everywhere that you also pretend to be everywhere outright? So, without any resistance to their whims and privileges, without anyone bothering them in their actions, without anyone troubling their conscience? They ask for too much. I don't think we'll reach an agreement.

—It would be more consistent with your ideas. If you left.

—No, absolutely not. I don't believe, as those words imply, that a country has ideological owners. Lobbies may have the power of a country and even the world, but that doesn't mean they own it by right. There are many decent people here, you know? If this country still has something democratic about it, it's not thanks to the lobbies that put and remove presidents, write their speeches, and impose their own decisions, but rather to those who don't believe all the sweetened lies that drip from the spheres of Wall Street and other less known and more perverse ghettos. Do you also want those of us who only have our independent or dissenting voice as our sole power to leave the most powerful country in the world to leave even the last free corner to you? What do you intend, that I leave you the little space that dissidents still have? Aren't you satisfied with everything you already have? No? It's in your nature, you always want more. It would be consistent for those who invade and support military, economic, and financial interventions in weaker countries to withdraw from each of those backward, violent, barbaric countries, in a word. However, no country in the world has so many interests and people involved in countries that are criticized and despised. If you criticize and despise them so much, why don't you leave? For my part, I can bother more here. Don't you think I bother? I even bother in the media where I'm invited, what greater honor could I have?

—That is, through programs like this. Say it outright.

—I don't intend to hide it. It's like this, power expresses itself and uses programs like this to feed the illusion of freedom for its consumers.

—In what other country would you be invited to give such insulting opinions against the one who invited you?

—Oh, undoubtedly in many. In fact, it's part of my job. There are many countries more democratic than this one. Others much less, and I haven't spared them criticism. But the truth is not a business, and I can't say that the oppressed and the oppressor share it equally. On the other hand, don't forget that in programs like yours, as in any other debate or pseudo-debate of ideas, some negative element like me is essential to leave the impression that those who own the system and the system itself are tolerant and democratic. But the truth is that only what doesn't threaten the system is allowed, and I in no way represent a threat but, on the contrary, to a certain extent serve that system by legitimizing it with my weak dissent. Moreover, out of simple gratitude for your kind invitation, I'm being honest with you. Now, if you don't want to hear it, if your platform is bothered by the truth, that's understandable, but it's not my responsibility.

—You're a cynic, a typical failed short-haired feminist —Lilí cut her off.

—Yes. Short hair on women, long hair on men is always a problem. But of all the labels, I prefer that of cynic. A cynic is the opposite of a hypocrite. A cynic is someone who has taken their criticism to the extreme, someone who no longer believes in official speeches, in the tears of good men and women who appear on television. That is, a cynic is a *hyper*-critic. The hypocrite, as the word says, is a *hypo*-critic, someone who has intentionally and conveniently suspended criticism. Which are the most abundant cases.

—I've heard a lot of nonsense in my career as a host, but never like this. I'm going to ask you very civilly to leave the studio. I won't tolerate disrespect of this magnitude.

Professor Ocampo stands up and as she leaves, they shout at her, "*¡communist, go home communist!*".

—When we return, we'll come back with something more constructive. Because our people have something more in their brains and hearts than hatred and resentment. The love of our people is what we see triumphing every day, making this country that opened its doors with affection even greater so they can achieve the long-awaited American dream.

Monday, April 20. Dow Jones: 7,841
Islamorada, Florida. 11:15 PM

Uncle Caíto was in his early thirties when they caught him in 1972. They say he had collaborated with some Tupamaros who were fugitives in the field where he worked.

I remember his receding hairline and his thick mustache. He still stuttered when he got nervous.

If he were alive, we'd probably be halfway through an argument, maybe over some political debate. Why did you get involved in that? How didn't you realize that the Russians also had their dictatorship, their own crimes, their own injustices, their own crap?

Of course, it's easy to think that now. How easy it is to fix the past. If only we could see where we're walking with the same clarity as we can see backward, where we can no longer do anything. But it's a human condition: we learn as we stop needing it. We learn to raise a child when that child has already grown up, or we truly understand a father when he's already an old man or no longer with us.

Uncle Caíto was caught in a field in Tacuarembó, Uruguay, and they dragged him with a horse as if his body were a plow. They tried to drown him several times in a stream. He couldn't confess anything because he knew less than the soldiers who wanted to know something, aside from having fun, because the days were long and the pay was meager.

Maybe Caíto made up a name or a place or a number to ease his pain for a moment.

In prison, he had to endure a lot. One visiting day, he confessed to his mother that he had become a Tupamaro in there. At least from then on, the military dictatorship had a serious reason to keep him.

Military justice must have had other reasons to use amusement and the pleasure of others' suffering, just as respectable spectators feel pleasure at the torture of an animal in a bullfight.

The soldiers back then were very creative when they were bored. Sometimes I've proposed the creation of a Museum of the Dirty War, as a monument to the human condition. But I've always been told that would be inconvenient, something that wouldn't help the understanding among all Uruguayans. Perhaps that's why there are many museums about the Charrúa Indians, where pots and little arrows of those friendly savages are displayed, but none about the Charrúa holocaust carried out by some heroes who still ride like multiplied ghosts on their bronze horses through the streets of various cities. I'm sure the material for such a museum would be very diverse, with so many declassified documents here and there (those sterile psychoanalytic confessions that democracies make every thirty years to ease their existential conflicts), with so many sex toys and other curiosities so educational for academics and students.

For example. One day the soldiers punished a prisoner and pretended they had castrated him. Then they passed by where Caíto was and showed him a kidney, a surgical container, full of blood.

—"Today we castrated this one," one of them said. "Tomorrow it's your turn."

The next day, Caíto's groin was monstrously swollen. He had spent the whole night trying to hide his testicles.

I learned about this story from some who had been with him. Then I remembered and understood why my grandmother Joaquina would tell someone, in secret, that they hadn't been able to find her son's testicles. As a child, I imagined that my uncle had a congenital defect and that's why he'd never had children.

They told Marta, his wife, something similar:

"Today we castrate him. Tomorrow we shoot him."

Of course, the soldiers of the homeland did neither one nor the other. They didn't go to such extremes because in Uruguay, the disappeared weren't as common as in Argentina or Chile. Uruguayans have always been more moderate, more civilized. More subtle. We've always felt so small between Brazil and Argentina and so relieved and proud not to reach the barbarities of our stepbrothers.

After all, if it's not talked about, it doesn't exist, as in *The House of Bernarda Alba*: "Silence, silence, silence, I said..."

Around that time, my brother and I were at the country house. I was three years old, and my brother was almost twice that. We were playing in the yard, next to the wheels of a cart, when we heard a very loud noise. I remember the yard, the cart, the tree, and almost everything else. We ran and got there before anyone else to Aunt Marta's room. Aunt Marta was lying on her back on the bed, with a hole in her chest.

Immediately, an adult dragged us outside to avoid the inevitable.

We were supposed to be traumatized, to become delinquents or something like that.

I don't know about the first part, but I can attest that the most lawless thing I've done in my life was when I was five years old. I climbed up the control tower of a prison and set off the alarms. After the commotion of security agents running below me, they brought me down, hanging by one arm. As a child, I also passed clandestine messages in the most secure prison in the country, thanks to my memory at the time, which my university friends would later praise.

Caíto died shortly after being released. Which is a figure of speech. He was imprisoned in the largest prison for political prisoners in a town called Libertad. Let's say, to be more precise, that he died in the middle of the countryside, shortly after leaving prison, at the age of 39. Maybe from a heart attack, as the doctor said, or from a blow to the head, as his mother thought, or from both. Or from all the other things.

If he were alive today, we'd probably be arguing over political reasons. Me, throwing his mistakes in his face. Him calling me a "petty bourgeois" or something equally deserved. Or maybe I'm wrong, and we'd still be as good friends as we were until he died.

Because, deep down, what matters most are not the political reasons. The sadism they exercised on him has no ideology, though it can eventually serve dictatorships of the left or the right, democracies of the North or the South.

The Caítos and Martas of Uruguay don't matter much. They weren't disappeared and died of natural causes or committed suicide. On the other hand, those soldiers with a sense of humor who played at castrating prisoners must now be poor old men who make sure their grandchildren don't watch violent scenes on TV, while explaining to them that the violence and lack of morality in society today is due to the loss of fundamental family values.

Tuesday, April 21. Dow Jones: 7,841
Aromas, California. 9:10 AM

Created in 1933 by Jerry Siegel and Joe Shuster, Superman is an alien. The savior, with biblical reminiscences— the parents place the child in a small ship and send it to another world—comes from the outside and aims "to change the destiny of a world." Here, "changing the destiny of a world" means the opposite: preventing the bad guys from changing it, preventing any kind of change, equating *evolution* with *revolution* and progress with the status quo. The split occurs when the symbol of the central culture is represented by a character coming from outside that same culture. What is represented and its representation are contradictory.

The visible face of the Moon, Clark Kent, is the image of his creators: both worked in newspapers, were shy, and had timid relationships with women. Lois Lane is one of those beautiful women who works near Clark Kent and underestimates him for his clumsiness and cowardice—

she repeatedly calls him a "coward"—while admiring Superman without limits.

If we analyze the first stories published massively and with unexpected success in 1939, we see a clear reflection of the Great Depression of the '30s, the communist threat, and the "socialist" politics of W. D. Roosevelt.

We can observe two planes of dislocation. 1) The feeling of frustration of the middle class and the idea of injustice in the working class. 2) The splitting of this frustration not to the detriment of the established power but to its benefit.

From the beginning, we see the feelings of the people who surrounded these two young men. Superman is the "Champion of the helpless and oppressed"[4] In the first story of his history, Superman helps a small businessman who struggles to keep his workers employed but faces the refusal of banks and the ambition of a stronger businessman who seeks to eliminate him from competition. Superman intimidates the banker and then repeatedly saves

---

[4] In the first strips, there are several spelling errors, despite being handwritten.

the modest man until he discovers the plan to assassinate him.

Superman is significantly presented as "The Man of Tomorrow," a kind of superman or the "New Man" of Che Guevara, the new socialist man who fights for the justice of the poor and helpless. The explicit reference to workers could have set off all the alarms if there had been a Senator McCarthy at the time: the red cape could be associated with communism, and the large S on his chest seemed too ambiguous between US (United States) and SU (Soviet Union). At the end of this story, when the beneficiary offers him a reward, Superman declares: *"My only desire is to see that the oppressed are assisted and the evil pay for their crimes"*.

This idea is confirmed in the story of the following week. *"The champion of the helpless and oppressed"*.

In Superman, the idea of (1) Evolution through (2) millions of years and of "another humanity" (the New Man) is explicit.

The dominant culture (1) stages its own flaws, injustices, and dissatisfactions to then (2) present a solution that does not question the origin of the problem. The reader will initially identify with the injustice portrayed, only to later psychologically accept the solution as a continuation of the diagnosis they accepted.

The reporter-investigator tries to solve the mystery of the disappearance of workers. It turns out that an evil scientist (the dark version of the sciences produced by the same comic world) "hypnotizes" the workers to make them produce more.

"*The men, helpless to protest, are forced to do back breaking labor...*" The importance of the issue is explicit when the editor of the Daily Planet dismisses the news of a bank robbery to focus attention on the disappearance of the workers.

Finally, a crowd prevents the hypnotized workers from committing suicide, an act of unquestionably good morals that is associated with the will of the system: the crowd is not the workers.

Here the first step appears: the comic presents the reality or suspicion of a system but splits it into an individual (the representative of the system) who can be eliminated (the solution) to maintain the questioned system. The opposite of *Modern Times* (1936), where the central character is the victim. Although it is a critique of dehumanization, as a character he is humanized, has an identity, and the viewer can identify with him. In Superman's case, the victims are always anonymous, while the avenger (the representative of the system, the defender of the weak who defends the oppressors of the weak) is the dehumanized character (a man of steel with superpowers) who, as a character, is humanized (he possesses an identity that, though dual, is familiar and known to the reader).

Similarly, we can see in Spanish and Latin American literature from colonial times: the king, the highest authority, is the source of complaints and justice; it is never questioned. The middle ranks are always questioned and accused of corruption or abuse of power. In Superman, we can also see a splitting or offloading: responsibility is inverted, shifting from the higher power to the intermediate or lower power.

This splitting is reinforced by the fact that there is no "logical," direct, or practical relationship between the forced labor of the workers and the attempted assassination of the governor. [on page 16, a vague explanation is given that links capital to political power. But the reasons for Ravek's attempt to assassinate the governor are never explained]

Here, science is negative because the world of Superman is a scientific-technological world.

Another splitting: When someone questions Superman's existence, they say, "*he must be a myth* (debe ser un mito)", at which point Superman retorts: "*I am a very material myth* (soy un mito muy material)".

Then look at page 16: "*...and Superman doesn't care to talk... he acts!*"

Saturday, May 2. Dow Jones: 8,212
Las Vegas, Nevada. 9:19 PM

The third-person narrator is what remains of literature, of traditional fiction, the fiction that knows it is fiction. The real fictions of today use the first person. The "I" in blogs, the "I" on Facebook, the "I" in photos. Above all, the "I." The ego of old artists pales in comparison to the democratic ego. It is not a collective ego but the collectivity of egos...

He was thinking about this and taking notes when he received an email from Luisa, one of his cousin Marcela's daughters. It was an invitation to accept her as a friend on Facebook. Well. He had initially created that account so no one would beat him to it and usurp his identity online, and in no time he had become trapped in the web. Not wanting to seem unfriendly to that girl he had barely had time to get to know, he accepted the invitation. But that girl was no longer a girl. He could hardly recognize her in a photo. Rather, he recognized her mother, Marcela. Below the smiling face, 458 photos from the same profile.

It was March 2; a snowstorm had broken out, forcing schools and offices to close. He left the melancholic snow-covered streets of Philadelphia. He clicked on Luisa's photo and confirmed it. Luisa, her sisters, brothers, making faces, lying on a summer bed, on the sands of Punta del Este, hitchhiking on, what was the name of the coastal road that leads into Punta from Piriapolis? Twenty years ago, he had gone to Montevideo to take an oral exam in structural calculus, and after passing it, sweating, he suggested to his brother that they go eat at a restaurant; and they went along the rambla and then the interbalnearia,[5] and then he doesn't remember a dark road until they reached that coastal road and entered Punta del Este, full of pretty girls, and Ernesto and his brother didn't dare to pick up the ones hitchhiking by the side of the road, out

---

[5] *Interbalnearia,* coastal highway

of sheer shyness, so they ended up parked next to a club where the comedian Ehrlich from Buenos Aires was telling jokes to a select audience, and Ernesto and his brother listened with the window open, eating a mortadella sandwich. Now that friendly girl is one of Marcela's daughters, as if she were a young Marcela, with a backpack on her shoulder and accompanied by two friends. Click. At a gathering of half-naked young people, drinking beer, telling high school stories or who knows what. In another, posing like her aunt Nina, with a cigar in one hand in the style of Marilyn Monroe, looking at a boy with prominent muscles, blond hair, skin tanned by the leisure work on the beach, undoubtedly upper class, smiling, happy, young, beer and pop, summer jokes, innocent teenage seductions, though perhaps it was his generation that was innocent, content with just flirting. And his brother Omar, the face of their father.

Ernesto was surprised. It had been five years since he left Uruguay, and all his cousins' children had left childhood behind for discos and teenage relationships. Their bodies had doubled in size, their faces were the faces of their parents, that is, Ernesto's cousins, with some variations. And their stories, and their joys would be the same with some variations. And Marcela and her sisters were now Aunt Rosa with some variations.

Suddenly Luisa inserts an old photo. An old photo! There are Marcela, Inés, Jaime, and Luisita as a baby. And those are the real faces and smiles that Ernesto remembers. Those are Ernesto's real cousins, Ernesto thinks. And there in the background is Aunt Rosa, the real Rosa at her real age. Why doesn't Ernesto recognize himself as almost forty, already forty, in his forties? Where did he get the idea that the real Ernesto is nineteen, or twenty-five, no older?

Saturday, May 9. Dow Jones: 8,574
Santa Fe, New Mexico. 6:15 PM
—We bring the word of the Lord. The Bible.

—Thank you, but I already have it.

—Very well. Will you invite us in? We'd like to read some pages.

—Do you know how to read?

—Yes, of course.

—I do too, thank you.

—Would you allow us into your home?

—No.

—Why not?

—You might be the nicest people in the world, but I can't let strangers into my home.

—But we bring the word of God.

—Anyone can say that, even a criminal.

—You can't confuse us with people possessed by the devil! Look into our eyes, what do you see? Do you see demonic people?

—I see very good people, with beautiful faces and very sweet stories.

—Then why do you doubt?

—Because according to the Scriptures, the devil is beautiful and speaks sweetly. To deceive, one must have many attributes.

—You insult us with your distrust. Your hatred won't let you open your heart to the Truth. Surely you're one of those who believe man descended from monkeys.

—No, I never believed that. Not even evolutionists believe in such inaccuracy. That man descended from monkeys is a confusion that comes from reggaeton. Still, I don't think you're demonic people. I just think you're mistaken, if not in your beliefs, at least in your method.

—You're condemning yourself to hell.

—Aren't you?

—We have been blessed and saved for all eternity…

—I suspect God deserves better.

—…and the Lord never changes His mind, because it is written here…

Friday, May 15. Dow Jones: 8,277
Casa Grande, Arizona. 4:00 AM

Susana, one of the flaws of our developed world is that it has become just that: a cage of lights and sounds that are increasingly repetitive and numbing. The lights blind, the noises deafen, and communication disconnects us.

Yesterday, a student knocked on my office door because he wanted to talk to me about a course. He was talking to himself, so I thought he must have been using one of those phones that many people have embedded in their brains on the right side of their ear. A new cyborg.

For a moment, I doubted whether he was actually talking to someone else while asking me about some texts he had to read for the week. Reaching the limit of my patience, I asked him if he was talking to me or to someone else.

"With both," he said.

I tried not to lose my civility and told him to disconnect or leave my office. To which he justified himself with the tale of the *multiple-task* generation.

"Oh, the Multi-Tasking Generation. Very well. Now, could you summarize the conversation we just had?

"Umm, so... Yes, you were talking to me about a text."

"What text?"

"Umm... I mean..."

I prolonged the silence on purpose.

Since the last century, we have been arguing about the historical opportunities for a radicalization of humanism through the expansion of education, culture, and the political and ideological power of the popular classes via new interactive communication systems. More and more often, I find myself disillusioned by these crude deviations from the supposed *conscientization* that Paulo Freire spoke of, from that sweet utopia of the liberation of powerless men and women through their labor and educational independence. More and more often, I experience the frustration that this liberation is as illusory as knowing someone through a "virtual society" like *Facebook*, where even emotions come prefabricated and packaged. The old vices of major television networks, such as indoctrination through propaganda, are also reproduced on the Internet. With the added problem that now the dependency has no schedule or economic barriers. All it takes is being *connected*.

With the added problem that now alienation confirms itself with the proud superstition of an individual finally liberated.

There is only one hope left: that those clumsy stammers, that entire alienation, is nothing more than the expression of an infantile stage preparing for a more mature one.

"OK, could you at least tell me what you were talking about with your friend?" I asked.

"Personal matters," he replied. Another prefabricated phrase.

"For personal matters, there's the cafeteria. Don't waste my time with Donald Duck theories. The Multi-Tasking Generation is nothing more than the fancy name for a Generation of Multiple Mutilations. Go, do something for humanity. Throw that hook in the trash. Grab a book, a newspaper, an apple, something your hands can feel. Go out and look at the moon. Turn off the lights in your apartment. Please, *sign out, log off, shut down and turn off.* Disconnect. Listen to silence a hundred and fifty times before coming back."

When the boy left, probably driving his Ford Explorer and typing on his iPod with his right thumb to some other *cyborg* in Japan or Spain about what had just happened with his professor, I realized that my annoyance had multiplied for another additional reason. The boy was a caricature of myself, of all of us, of the new anonymous society of blind insects that will die embraced by the fire of the lights.

Then I disconnected and went out to breathe.

Friday, May 15. Dow Jones: 8,277
Casa Grande, Arizona. 4:00 AM
I had always dreamed that this day would come, and it finally became a reality. Every time I dreamed of it, I woke up crying, and when I realized it had only been a dream, I couldn't stop thinking about the same thing. I would think and think before getting up, and I always ended up, as an adult, killing all those pigs who had done it. Then I would tell myself it had all been a dream and that the rest was just a product of my imagination. But I

also knew that it would happen someday, though I didn't dare to call it by its name so it wouldn't happen.

And yet it happened. It was at night, just like in my dreams, and for a moment I thought it was a dream. I don't know where the bomb exploded or if it was one or a thousand bombs that went off at the same time, and I barely had time to think that this wasn't a dream when the ceiling began to creak and collapsed on us.

All our upstairs neighbors died, and of my family, only my sister and I survived. Though I wish a thousand times I hadn't survived to see my sister like this, crawling in a pool of black blood and now like this, looking at everything with one eye that barely moves. To see the letters she writes, she has to bring her little eye very close to the paper, and to look when someone speaks to her, she has to turn her whole head and then her entire body because the eye doesn't move. And the doctors say that fortunately, the eyelid can go up and down, because otherwise, that little eye wouldn't be saved either, and she'd be blind. And God has allowed enough suffering by letting the bombs prevent her from walking due to her broken back and not preventing her from remembering that mom, dad, and all the siblings who were sleeping there that night died just before sunrise. And to avoid more trouble, my grandfather sent me back to my aunt's.

Because I'm also dead, and that's why it won't cost me anything to do what I have to do, like any good son or any good brother. I'll only have peace when I fulfill my duty.

Friday, May 15. Dow Jones: 8,277
Casa Grande, Arizona. 4:55 AM

It's not true that I'm a disrespectful skeptic. I'm respectful. I deeply respect the image of a Virgin crying blood. Because I respect those who believe it's a miracle and those who believe in the Virgin. I even respect the possibility that such a phenomenon is a miracle, and I respect the probability, however slim, that the Virgin would concern herself with such things.

I respect, but I'm not concerned. Much more than a plaster Virgin crying or sweating blood, I'm concerned with the hand of a manager firing a thousand people under the irrefutable excuse of budget cuts. I'm concerned with laws that better respect the rights of dogs to a dignified life than the rights of an immigrant family to be treated, if not as humans, at least like those dogs. I'm concerned and care much more about the hand of a tyrant signing a war, the feet of a fanatic ascending to heaven. I suspect that God, the Virgin, and their servants might agree with me. At least on this. Of course, only they would know. I don't know, nor do the fanatics who nervously climb to their private heavens on staircases of the dead, always so sure of what they say and do.

Monday, May 25. Dow Jones: 8,277
Boca Raton, Florida. 9:30 AM

The paradox of Captain America, Susana, lies in another duality. Like all popularized heroes, he is the result of another scientific experiment that wasn't sufficiently controlled. The intention was to create "Supersoldiers," truly perfect humans—which is another paradox if we consider the nature of these dehumanized men by the simplification of the myth—rooted in physical and martial superiority. Captain America primarily fights against the Nazis, who, in reality, explicitly promoted the idea and practice of the same experiment of the superior man through their (primitive) physical and dominant capabilities.

Perhaps you can continue with other classic characters. Don't forget the television years.

Tuesday, May 26. Dow Jones: 8,305
El Dorado, Arkansas. 10:30 AM

When they knocked on the door and my daddy stepped back saying in a low, worried voice that it was immigration, mom let out a little scream of fright that was muffled between her two hands pressed to her face. Daddy wanted to hide her, but she refused so he wouldn't be put in jail for lying. So they opened the door and were talking very quietly, but one voice sounded harsh. You could hear closet doors, people going in and out of the bathroom and kitchen. Then the noises and shadows were no longer heard, and I thought it was all over. After a while, I heard them saying okay, many okays, and mom came back to my room to give me a kiss, and I never saw her again. She was smiling, but now I know she didn't want to smile and only smiled so I'd remember her like that, as I always remember her.

So dear teacher, if you want a three-hundred-word composition in Spanish about my country, you'll have to give me a D or an F because right now I can't think of anything else.

Tuesday, May 26. Dow Jones: 8,305
Soledad, California. 11:30 AM

Yes, of course. We could start with the adorable Hulk. I'm not talking about the original, which seemed more like a scrawny parody. The one played by Lou Ferrigno was more mature.

Let's begin. Hulk is the spirit of King Kong now manifesting in another form of dislocation. It's no longer the civilization-barbarism dislocation but the dislocation of the individual alienated from mechanical civilization. Like all characters in the mythical-comic genre, the manifestation of terror and justice are products of a scientific experiment. Science is no longer the paradigm of truth it was in the 19th century but the new nature of mechanical civilization that produces monsters. At the same time that science produces popular heroes, it is responsible for the world's evil. Dr. Jekyll and Mr. Hyde, Frankenstein, Terminator, Hulk, The Nuclear Man, the Bionic Woman, etc.

Like the English story of duality, Bill Bixby is a doctor, a representative not only of rationality but of science. The beast, expression of the irrational, is now a positive agent. Like the previous heroes, justice is achieved through violent, muscular explosion.

If in Superman, the character of the journalist-investigator is a positive figure, in Hulk the journalist-investigator represents an oppressive society that pressures the individual until he explodes in fury. As in the original Superman series, each episode was preceded by the presentation and explanation of the hero. The audience knows him well, but it's necessary to link this "being" to the situation of each scene. The previous announcement always repeats:

"And now when Dr. David Banner becomes enraged, a horrifying metamorphosis occurs […] The anger drives the creature that is pursued by an inquisitive reporter."

Bill Bixby: *"Mr. McGee, don't provoke me, I'm not myself when I'm angry"*.

"The monster is accused of a murder he didn't commit. David Banner has disappeared. He wants to make the world think he's dead until he can control the violent spirit that lives within him".

In the dislocation, the visible face of the Moon has become illegal, and like the doctor in *The Fugitive*, Dr. David Banner wants to disappear, *"make the world think he's dead until he can control the violent spirit that lives within him"*.

Hulk is an asexual hero because he is entirely associated with sexual activity. Bill Bixby becomes Hulk when he is aroused by an act of injustice. This feeling is opposed to eroticism and produces the muscular-phallic multiplication that unleashes its rage against the provocateur.

Like in Superman, Hulk integrates the tradition of the detective-journalist, but in this case, the inquisitor has switched "to the other side."

Look here, because in the '60s there's a shift in these stories.

Friday, May 29. Dow Jones: 8,500
Cocoa, Florida. 4:35 PM
The problem with the judge isn't that she's a woman or that she's Hispanic, as they want to say. It's that phrase from October 26, 2001, at the University of California, Berkeley. You know, if instead of "better" she had said "different," it would be another story. We wouldn't be discussing her nomination to the Supreme Court today. No, it's not that I remember it by heart, it's recorded. She said that a Latina woman, more precisely "a wise Latina woman" with the richness of her experience could more often than a "white male" reach a better conclusion, so,

that is, a "better conclusion" than a white man who had never lived that life. You see, if we just change that word, we'd have a statement that wouldn't hurt her chances of getting our vote as much. Yes, that phrase. Look, it would be very clear and very clean: *"I would hope that a wise Latina woman with the richness of her experiences would more often than not reach a* different *conclusion than a white male who hasn't lived that life"*. Don't you think? Impeccable. But with that word in the middle, *better, better,* I don't think Judge Sonia Sotomayor can represent us all equally, I don't think she's capable of applying the law in its technical form. Look, a judge must have the ability to interpret the law, not the temptation to make it, because that's what we, the representatives of the people, are here for. And with this phrase, it has been proven that the judge has an agenda. Well, it's not that I support the claims of Rush Limbaugh or Congressman Newt Gingrich, accusing her of being racist as well. Maybe a little sexist, but I'm not sure about racist, because, look, deep down we Latinos know that in the history of the Supreme Court there have been some women, but no representative of our Latino community. Excuse me? Eight? Well, I didn't know that fact, but if really eight out of the ten most debated

nominees belonged to some minority, that's pure coincidence. Let's not overinterpret a coincidence. But of
course, the race, color, or gender of the candidate isn't that
important, because it's about applying the law technically,
and in this country, we don't have discriminatory laws of
any kind. Well, Mr. Journalist, the issue of gay marriages
is still unresolved, and there are many conflicting opinions. No, I'm not against civil rights and liberties; on the
contrary, you know my record in Congress, but the problem is how we define marriage and parenthood. Personally, I don't agree with reinterpreting history to push a
political agenda. No, it's not that I give too much importance to words. You know I'm a man of ideas, and
more than ideas, of concrete actions. But on the other
hand, it would be an act of arrogance to try to change the
word of God for outdated reasons. And God is the Word,
and that's why we must be careful when we interpret or
make laws that are, essentially, words of authority, words
to be respected beyond the whims of each generation.
Otherwise, we wouldn't have the oldest constitution in
the world, look.

Saturday, May 30. Dow Jones: 8,500
Paso Robles, California. 3:30 PM

Another is *The Fugitive*. Do you remember this character? Richard Kimble is sentenced to death for a crime he didn't commit. Sound familiar? In this case, the protagonist is accused of killing his own wife. To flee in search of true justice, he dyes his hair black. He rejuvenates; in black and white, blond and gray are the same. Kimble must take on multiple jobs, always hiding his true identity, always evading the police. It's the exact reproduction of the illegal immigrant. But this expression of collective desire—the escape—embodied in a kind doctor, unjustly suspected of a crime, doesn't aim for consumption or production but the opposite. It's the exaltation of the frugality of the '60s and freedom at the same time, although in a real situation it would mean the exact opposite. It's not the countercultural frugality of the hippies. It's the kidnapping and subsequent neutralization of the same irresponsible desire for frugality, for renunciation, of the feeling of injustice from a power that fails to satisfy. The desire that threatens reality is realized symbolically, fully in fantasy, like forbidden sex, the infidelity of a faithful husband who dreams. Injustice has triumphed, and there's no end in sight, like in Vietnam. *"Victim of blind justice"* (image of justice and the scales)

Music and myth also colonize the sensitivity of the spectators from the colonized periphery. Distant men and women sympathize with the individual outside their own context. *The Fugitive* is understood as a fantasy, a product of pure imagination. Therefore, innocent. The expression of a frustration. The innocent insult to power, to dominant justice. In short, a reparative fantasy.

Thursday, June 4. Dow Jones: 8,750
La Canada, California. 6:10 PM

I never dreamed I'd end up living a stone's throw from Beverly Hills, though I always told Ricardo, because it's known that when you repeat a desire enough, it ends up coming true. Ricardo mocked my aspirations and started playing with that baby-drink-see-baby-fool thing, like a dumb Berber.

He underestimated me. He thought that because my father was a modest greengrocer, I had no right to have ambitions in life and to progress. My father was a green-grocer, but not just any greengrocer. In Santa Cruz, we had a chain of stands that employed more than ten cholos.

Until one day everything started going wrong because of the usual troublemakers who filled their heads with racist ideas, and we blue-eyed Cruceños became foreigners in our own country. And to be honest, I wasn't going to spend my whole life surrounded by tomatoes and stone-faced people chewing coca leaves.

Here I did very well at first, except for the last year. But I have hope that everything will return to normal. At least here one can hope that things will go back to normal and not be fed up with the normal and tired of waiting for the utopias that never come.

In a few weeks, the tent city of Sacramentillo was dismantled, and we came with Ricardo with the promise and the hope that it would only be for a few days until Obama would get the debtors out of the *foreclosures* and return to us the house in Santa Barbara that had cost us so much. Ricardo said it hadn't cost us much because we hadn't even paid three percent, but I didn't care because the gentlemen who sold it to us with all the sweet talk sold us a plan we could afford with Ricardo's salary. But when the payments went up like crazy and we couldn't pay for a few months, they kicked us out with the dog and everything. And we left everything on the street. We weren't going to bring the jacuzzi. The brand-new TV we had bought wouldn't even fit in this tent. We saved the two cars, though the insurance is about to expire, and we gave the dog to the American woman who lived next door. She got lucky because she did what she had to do on time, and she didn't go around like me, worrying about the image and the morality of the house, so Ricardo could show off every time he invited his boss or one of his clients over for dinner. Someone who sells life insurance has to show and prove that they live well, and on that we agreed. But in the end, Marilyn fared better than me. At least she's still there, I was told, in her palace, with her parties and her clients who, she says, only go to buy glove and purse designs. Maybe it's because Americans always know how to do it better, even when they do it wrong.

One evening, before Ricardo came back from work, I made sure to smash as much as I could with a hammer, because no one was going to enjoy all the improvements we had made to that dream mansion that was stolen from us. When Ricardo arrived, he didn't say anything. He just stared at the destroyed walls and furniture and said, "ok," which is sometimes like saying nothing. He had also been acting strange for days—I don't know if he was drowning his sorrows in whiskey or in Marilyn's arms. He didn't argue anymore, didn't smile or cry, he acted as if I didn't exist. That's not the whiskey's doing, I thought, but a Marilyn with those red lips and cheerful cleavage. I must admit the damned woman had a better body than me. To clear my doubts, I would send Ricardo to Marilyn's house to complain that her bushes were invading our *backyard*. I'd time him and realize he was taking longer than necessary. It wasn't hard to imagine during those unnecessary minutes that milky-white, slippery little body, like a woman's desire, being caressed by Ricardo's gaze and her always cheerful, thick, red, and shiny smile driving men crazy, stealing their sleep. When Ricardo returned, I did everything I could to show him I had noticed, that I wasn't a fool, and that's why I wasn't going to say anything, so he could prepare himself, because those who live by the sword die by the sword.

Later I found out about the *foreclosure* and I went crazy for a day. But only for a day.

The good thing about Sacramentillo is the evenings when some idle neighbors come over to chat for a while. We gather our sorrows and memories of the good times in Santa Barbara. Robert, for example, worked as a manager at Google, and overnight he was left searching, he says. He was less lucky than Ricardo. Joshua's woman left him because she said she'd rather die than come to a campsite, even if it was just for ten days while her parents sent her money from Massachusetts. And it seems the woman got the money and went to live alone in a hotel, and who knows what she's living on, but the truth is she's not going to show up here, let alone to see Joshua's face. The poor guy, he comes here every evening. When Robert isn't lurking around.

I learned to enjoy the beer that's never missing in Sacramentillo. It always seemed like a vulgar drink, for lowlifes, as Rosalía used to say in Santa Barbara. That's how I get back at this unjust world. I get back at the bad rich people by drinking beer, I get back at Ricardo for not wanting to switch to a better job in time that would have allowed us to move far away from Marilyn. He said he preferred security, and I told him his secure little job was going to lead us to this. God punished him for his dalliances with Marilyn, for all his lies. And He punished me for not reacting in time and still staying by the side of a fool. And I also get back at him because I no longer need to be a great lady or care about appearances. And I get back at

Heather, Joshua's woman, for thinking she's better than the rest of the women in Sacramentillo just because she has a master's degree in education and hasn't lost her job at the high school yet. But a job isn't everything in life, as everyone now believes since the world has turned upside down and women support their husbands who cheat on them while they break their backs and think they're the heroines of a world in crisis. Before all my youth is gone, before the cold of winter comes and wrinkles my eyelids, I'm going to enjoy the little I have left.

Thursday, June 4. Dow Jones: 8,750
Boca Raton, Florida. 7:05 PM
Susana, for my age, *The Six Million Dollar Man* was more important than *The Fugitive*. In its original version, it was called *The Six Million Dollar Man* (1974-1978). In Latin America, it was known as *El hombre nuclear*, and in Spain, the translation was more literal: *El hombre de los seis millones de dólares*.

In the '70s, we already have the cyborg consolidated, the man who is half man and half machine. After watching and admiring this series starring Lee Majors, as children we dreamed of having some mechanical part of our body that could perform some feat. This dehumanization of the human body is also a mechanization of the culture and civilization of the 20th century.

Most of the enemies of this man-machine are androids or complete machines that aim to replace or fight against humans. The dislocation lies in the fact that the awareness of the mechanization of the human is justified or hidden by the fact of fighting against the complete product of that same mechanical and spiritless culture.

In the movie "The Six Million Dollar Man vs. Bigfoot," the Six Million Dollar Man asks a kind of giant snowman. The primitive appearance of this man makes the Six Million Dollar Man ask: "Are you a man?". The man-machine doubts the humanity of a primitive, violent man. After an equally primitive struggle, the Six Million Dollar Man tears off the arm of the caveman, which turns out to be a complete machine. The man-machine reveals himself as human in the face of the machine-machine.

The Eve of this cyborg Adam is also a woman reconstructed and "enhanced" by science and technology. Her only limitation lies in the fact that after the accident and the implantation of superpowers, she cannot remember the past. The most significant forgetting is the forgetting of the Six Million Dollar Man's love, and every time she tries to remember or is about to recover her past (that is, her love), she suffers severe headaches. The Bionic Woman has no past, like a machine that has forgotten the history of previous inventions and the history of its human inventors.

The split here occurs when the symbol of the human, the hero who fights for the good of humanity, is represented by a character identified by his non-human functions (the cyborg). *What is represented and its representation are contradictory, which produces a displacement of meaning.*

Sunday, June 14. Dow Jones: 8,799
El Cajon, California. 1:30 AM

June 13 will go down as a historic date in the gang, and I don't know if one day we'll change the name and instead of Mara Jaguares 07, it will be called Jaguares J-13. The old lady loses this because of her inability to understand the real world, but one day soon she'll have to eat dust when I'm the number one of the Jaguares. It's not that I want to erase Bola, who until now is untouchable, and I respect him for what he did for the gang some time ago. Bola isn't the strongest or the bravest in the gang he inherited from Loca. Dodo is twice as strong as Bola, but no one messes with Bola, until now no one has been able to take the top spot in the gang. Bola would drive a nail into his sister's eyes to save the gang. Especially because his sister hates Bola for the son he had with her and made Loca abort. Bola says it's because of jealousy. The sister is always a danger to the gang, but she's his sister, and Bola might still care for her a little, but nothing stops Bola if the gang is in danger. After Loca and before the gang was rebuilt by Bola, no one had until now more awareness and, above all, guts to say and do what he says. Bola has taught us a lot about what it means to be men in the land of parking meters, something that only a few of us can understand, and that's why the new recruits are so eager to join. Not just anyone can be a Jaguar. The others exist in their dreams of prayers and the cheap talk of professors who make the guys in schools dumb and weak, all lacking the knowledge that the gang members have of the world because they live and are creators of the world of the streets and the basements of the city. Bola receives the information, listens to every report sent in an audio file to his iPod, and decides who can sell here and how many whores can hunt for clients on a corner that belongs to the gang. No one knows that everything seen on the streets is the result of our decisions. They live without knowing. They live because we let them live. They make money because of us, and so on.

But Bola is not forever and has his weaknesses.

On February seventh, Bola came to congratulate me on my mark in the gang, which will last for years to come and surely more if I take care to follow my own path. Or it's betrayal, but in Bola's time, which has been almost ten years, the gang hasn't grown as Loca would have wanted. And it was Loca, not Bola, who brought me from the Contra, because of my experience in the war. It was Loca, and because of Loca, maybe I would be the one in the gang if they hadn't killed him so early in prison. They say it was because of Bola. That Bola gave the order because of his sister's abortion, I mean, because of his son. After that, neither his sister, who died later, nor Bola himself could father more children, they say it was God's punishment. And Bola slept with half a million girls to prove he could still have heirs, and nothing, absolutely nothing, they say none of them got pregnant after the abortion. And because of that, Bola got revenge on Loca in the fourth year of Loca's jail time, and by the way, he got rid of the annoying commands of the One who was no longer the One by that time.

I remember that Loca used to say every time we gathered for drinks that he wanted to die in the streets, in action, and not in prison, but it didn't happen. And I always hoped he would repeat in front of the Jaguars that I was his favorite, despite my age, because I had experience in the jungle. But Bola convinced the others that the jungle and the asphalt were not the same, which is confusing because a man's worth is proven anywhere. Another difference was that Bola had to strangle the dog of the initiates in order to join the gang, and when I joined, I already had dead men and women I couldn't count on my hands. But out of modesty, I let the gangsters and wannabes here who spoke English also give orders, and that was my weakness—not asserting myself from the start—and so I kept paying the price of a beginner when I wasn't a beginner, and many could have learned from me.

But on the seventh, everyone learned who Chucho is, that it wasn't just stories I brought from the jungle but the courage many lack to be inside.

I calculated that for two years Bola had been trying to reclaim Gallery Street and the three blocks that border the train tracks, and he had never succeeded. About three plans failed, but so many disasters didn't convince the gang that Bola wasn't hitting the mark, and the last time I had to somewhat disobey Bola's order not to risk another failure because it could cost us dearly, and I sent the Jaguars against the train line, right in alley 11 where the Fox blacks were celebrating the initiation of a new member, and without giving them time to sober up from the beer, I took out the new guy, a black kid taller than me but with a fear of killing, a fear of a black man but not of the Fox blacks who are the toughest I know, but a fear of a black man of milk, and I plunged the discipline blade, which is five inches long, into his stomach and left the poor guy writhing there. Maybe because the blacks didn't care much about the new member or because they didn't have the guts to respond to my stab since they saw me fully decided to kill or die, and they disappeared like crows.

It's true that the beer played in my favor, but the others in the gang saw this as a strategic move. What was truly strategic was making them believe what they had believed at first. The blacks backed off, and I took the opportunity to cut off one of the ears of the black guy who was still mumbling words, and I told him not to waste his breath because I didn't understand black English. I cut off the disgusting ear and put it in Robin's hands, who, with a look of surprise and fascination, took the ear and put it in his pocket for Bola.

Bola praised the feat, and that night we had a celebration, a first-class celebration, for honors. And Bola didn't bother to praise the exemplary bravery of one of his members or the achievement of the Jaguars in reclaiming all the blocks up to the railroad tracks. But I know deep down Bola looked at me with distrust. He would have wanted to have done it himself instead of me, and that's why he celebrated it as an achievement of the Jaguars instead of putting it in truthful terms, because I had done it all by myself, and the others had only followed the command.

One day when I'm the one, we're going to cross the train tracks and beyond, and the whole city will know who the Jaguars are and who Chucho is. Even in the gangs of the rival Cholitos neighborhood, they'll hear about Chucho and realize they lost back when I wanted to join the Mara Salvadora and they told me I wasn't worth a dime.

Tuesday, June 16. Dow Jones: 8,504

Atascadero, California. 8:30 PM

Dear Ernesto, since you've mentioned *The Six Million Dollar Man*, I can't help but continue with the governor. Let's see. The machine has taken the center of power. This apocalyptic idea is a culmination or perhaps just a logical continuation of the process that began in the 19th century. The world of humans is on the verge of extinction and has been completely relegated to the margins of power. Now the hero is a rebel who organizes the resistance.

It's the consciousness of the imperial world that feels threatened by a world as diverse as it is chaotic.

Sarah, the mother of the child who announces liberation, triumphs and flees to Mexico, just as Mary fled to Egypt. But in this world, there is no God. God is the great absence in the stories of dislocation. First, He is replaced by nature, and later by the machine.

Monday, June 15. Dow Jones: 8,652
Salida, Colorado. 3:25 PM

He stood against the blue wall and thought, "now the same old story begins." The photographer said,

—One more time.

Again and again. Ernesto could see the flash as it came out of the camera, and before it returned to the view-finder, he lowered his eyelids.

It always happened the same way. After the thirteenth time, the official ordered him to close his eyes. This variation was new to him. He thought they had finally found a way around his flaw this time.

—Open them now!

When he opened his eyes, the official had already fired, the flash had already left the machine, Ernesto had already seen the camera, the flash, and the serious face of the Motor Vehicle Division official, and he had closed his eyes again before the machine could notice.

On the nineteenth attempt, the official, visibly annoyed, said, "enough." Thank you.

As he crossed the sliding door, Ernesto glanced at his new driver's license. His face, the face he had always disliked, appeared with his eyes closed. One slightly more closed than the other.

As if winking.

Wednesday, June 16. Dow Jones: 8,612

Opa Locka, Florida. 6:25 AM

El Nuevo Herald of Miami. The Associated Press. Washington. *An animal rights organization wants President Barack Obama to show a more compassionate attitude the next time a fly bothers him at the White House.*

The organization People for the Ethical Treatment of Animals (PETA) sent the president a device that allows users to catch flying insects in their homes and release them outside.

"We are in favor of compassion, even for the most annoying, small, and unpleasant animals," said Bruce Friedrich, PETA's spokesperson, on Wednesday. "We believe that people, when they can be compassionate, should be so with all animals."

On Tuesday, irritated by the incessant buzzing of a fly during a televised interview at the presidential residence, the president decided to take justice into his own hands. Obama told the fly, "Get out of here," but the insect refused. Then, Obama waited for the fly to land, raised his hand, and crushed it on the first try. As if nothing had happened, the president asked CNBC journalist John Harwood, "What were we talking about?"

The U.S. president took a second to boast about the feat. "Impressive, huh?" said Obama. "I got the bug."

The cameras kept rolling in the East Room of the White House. Obama didn't even flinch. He pointed at the dead insect and asked, "Do you want to film it?".

CNBC did it, and the dead fly went down in history.

Friedrich said that PETA is pleased with Obama's voting record in the Senate in favor of animal rights and recalled that the president has spoken out vehemently against abuse in this area.

But "killing a fly on TV shows that he's not perfect," said Friedrich.

Friday, July 3. Dow Jones: 8,295

Espanola, New Mexico. 3:35 PM

On Sunday the 28th, Ricardo wrote to me from Tegucigalpa with overflowing joy. Finally, the monster Mel Zelaya has been ousted. He didn't even have time to set up a single ballot box for his ill-conceived little poll. The media, without exception, the parliament unanimously, the

Supreme Court collectively, and our glorious Armed Forces have dragged the pig out of his bed, put him on a plane, and left him all alone at the airport in Costa Rica. Ricardo's euphoria isn't contagious, Ernesto confessed to Lupe. It's frightening. The glorious Armed Forces have restored constitutional order, he shouted at me over the phone, they've brought peace and decency back to Honduras. What peace? Goodnight, Ernestito, and may God remove the blindfold from your eyes. I have to leave you now because tomorrow I have to get up early to work for this country. And he hung up. I also work for that country, Guadalupe complained. Don't forget the money I send every month. Taxes on exile, and with no return, Ernesto commented. The next day, in case it wasn't clear, Ricardo put it in writing in an email. Ernesto reads each of these words with sadness. Order, Peace, Decency, Family, Homeland. He hesitates to respond. He responds. Ricardo replies that only traitors can read with sadness, listen with concern to words of such value. Proof that the democratic process initiated by the glorious Armed Forces of Honduras, in defense of the Homeland, is on the right track. He doesn't care that no country in the world recognizes the coup, because it wasn't a coup, it wasn't a coup! It wasn't a coup! It wasn't a coup! shouts the new de facto president Roberto Micheletti to his supporters. Don't try to clarify, it only makes it worse, says Ernesto. Ricardo proudly raises his little flag. Thousands of protesters in favor of Micheletti. A few hundred in favor of Zelaya. Of course, Ricardo, the first group is summoned and protected by the glorious Armed Forces. The second group is repressed with batons and tear gas. You don't need to tell me, I've seen it live on the internet. Damn, outsiders don't get to have an opinion. Only those of us who live here, who suffer Honduras's problems, know what reality is. But, Ricardo, the Hondurans who support the elected government of Zelaya also live there and have a different opinion. What do you know, Ernesto? It's no coincidence that all those who support the bastard Mel Zelaya are poor, uneducated, with no judgment of their own, says Ricardo. Sometimes a phrase is worth a thousand words, says Ernesto. And Ricardo, without saying that their friendship and kinship are over, replies that the one responsible for the violence, poverty, and drug trafficking in Honduras is the populist donkey Mel, which is why, says Ernesto, there should be a coup in every country in this world. Obama also condemned the coup. Hey! Don't come at me now, that little black guy doesn't understand anything, said Ortez Colindres, the new chancellor. Rodríguez Zapatero should go back to his shoes, he also said. And that he wouldn't comment on El Salvador's position because it's not worth talking about such a small country, where you can't even play soccer because the ball lands in another country. Hey, that's decency, right? Don't come at me with your irony. Just look at all those in Hugo Chávez's little club, from Chile to Guatemala, and now the United States too. You'd better stay enjoying the honey of the Empire. Honduras doesn't need rats like you. And if the whole world has reached such a level of moral corruption that they can't understand the problems we face here every day, then we'll close all the doors of our beloved Homeland to defend with more conviction than ever our Honor and Morality. The fewer, the better. And you, little lackey, stay out of politics. Better stick to literature. Send whatever you have to Marino's contest. He knows me. The only condition, you know, something easy to read. Something neat, with a beginning, middle, and end, and well-drawn characters. Nothing weird, nothing that scares normal readers like me. If you don't have anything to send, keep writing those little stories you're so good at. Nobility obliges, and I must admit you have talent for that. In fact, I'll be blunt and say you're a real genius at it. But don't get carried away. That's it. Keep going down that path if you want to succeed. When you mix politics into your fantasies, you screw up, definitely. You become just another rat. Polish, perfect your fantasies. Stick to your knitting. Dedicate yourself to that. Reality is a man's business.

Saturday, July 11. Dow Jones: 8,141
Laguna Niguel, California. 4:10 PM.

I never went to *Moon Over Amtrak*. It seemed to me, and still does, an indecency. Father Rivero says it's more than an indecency—it's a tribute to the devil.

One day I went. That was five years ago. Since neither the mayor nor the police could stop it, I decided to go and preach in front of all those people who were eagerly waiting for the train to drop their pants and lift their skirts. I thought that even if I wasn't going to save a soul, at least I'd make them uncomfortable enough to ruin their fun. I had planned to keep an annual statistic, since the newspapers said it was on the rise ever since a small group of crazies started the tradition over twenty years ago. It all began with two kids betting to moon the train for a beer, Father Rivero told me. Two kids and two minor sins. The issue wasn't that big of a deal. If it had stayed between the two kids, it wouldn't have become a mortal sin. But today there are thousands, and everyone remembers the first two, because like fire, small sins spread until they become a blaze. It's not the little flame's fault, says the father, but the spread. And against this, we must fight our whole lives.

Almost at the beginning, when people were starting to gather against the wire fence that borders the train tracks, I saw her arrive.

It was Lilian. She came alone. The last thing I thought was that she would participate in all this. Having her close and having Nicole Kidman with her perfume must be the same. They're identical. With Father Rivero, I watched *Dead Calm* and had to turn my face away several times. The father likes ships, pirate stories, Peter Pan, and all that. I watched that movie almost sideways, and even then, I couldn't forget Kidman, even though Father Rivero thought I was born to be a priest and maybe even a bishop or cardinal because I didn't like women. And I never confessed to him that I loved Kidman almost naked in the ship's hold.

Lilian is as saintly and sinful as Nicole Kidman, with those deep eyes beneath that clear forehead. The prettiest girl in college, the most educated, the one who lived in Palo Alto in a three-level house. They say three levels not counting the basement. I knew her family was religious, and so was she, and for a moment I thought she would join my project.

She appeared with her contagious smile and asked me the time. I got the impression she thought I was just another one of those crazies, and it took me a while to realize she was there for the same reason. What surprised me most was the naturalness with which she spoke. It seemed like she knew some of the other crazies. They took it like someone who has a coffee and talks about global warming.

When the time came, I didn't know what to do. Or I didn't have the courage to do the right thing. I was paralyzed, and she was leaning against the fence that separates Camino Capistrano from the train tracks, looking at me with those sky-like eyes and smiling as if we were old accomplices in something. I was the one who thought of her every night. She was the one who dragged me into the fire of sin every dawn, unable to sleep. I went down to the ship's hold, and she couldn't resist. I'll never know if she ever thought of me. I can't even imagine her wasting her nights like that.

But that time, it was her who was looking at me. She looked at me and smiled, thinking about how beautiful she was and how much she could make me suffer, like a goddess makes her most devoted followers suffer.

I stood there mute like a statue of salt, petrified by her complicit gaze among the crowd of sinners waiting for the train like they wait for the ball to drop in New York on December 31st. But here it's always hot, very hot, that sinful California heat. And her against the fence, like a gun-slinger with her hands ready at the sides of her white skirt and the rumbling of the approaching train like a wave that never stopped growing in its delirium. And her, unmoving, always looking at me and smiling amidst the others who didn't notice that our gazes were linked by a ten-thousand-volt magnet.

The magnet broke when the train passed, and she bent down to lift her skirt over her back. I saw nothing but her

Nicole Kidman face, with that worldly happiness that has led many astray.

I don't remember anything else from that day. I think she disappeared, or I left without looking for her.

At college, we never mentioned anything. Actually, she never spoke to me again. She only showed up occasionally. When we crossed paths, she made that gesture they do here, something like a friendly smile, but those of us who've lived here for a long time know it's just a gesture that fades as soon as you pass by. It wasn't that complicit smile, that authentic gaze.

In the fall, she started dating a very popular guy from Palo Alto. She graduated in the spring and was immediately accepted into Duke University. I thought I wouldn't see her again and thanked heaven for freeing me from Lilian.

The second summer, I returned with the same intentions, and to my surprise, she did too. The same story as the previous summer. All my courage and determination crumbled like a house of cards. And again, her smile, her gaze, the ten-thousand-volt magnet, my clumsiness in resisting a demon who seemed like a fallen angel. And again, the same thing.

The third and fourth years passed the same way. The few words we exchanged were to confirm to her that I hadn't been able to get into any graduate school but was still studying at the seminary, and to inform me that she was about to finish her master's and had already been accepted to pursue a doctorate in Germanic languages.

Today is the fifth year I'm going to *Moon Over Amtrak*, and I hope it's the last. Maybe it's a way to end this. This time I've taken the train. This time she won't see me. At times I think it's a mistake. What I want most is for her to see me, what I want most is to look into her eyes, her smile. And for her to see me. At times I imagine I'll do everything I can to make her see me, but I know it's going to be impossible. I hope when the train passes, she doesn't smile at anyone else. I hope she thinks of me, that I didn't come this year.

I hope she realizes that this time I'm on the train.

Saturday, July 11. Dow Jones: 8,146
Altavista, Virginia. 9:19 AM
If there was one thing Ernesto couldn't stand about his life in the United States, it was running into some chauvinist who, with every word and every silence, showed his

conviction that Americans were "the good guys," the new chosen people to whom one had to be grateful for every invasion and every intrusion, political or military, into some barbaric, peripheral country, with the noble intention of saving them and giving them a lesson in democracy.

Apparently, this problem didn't just affect Ernesto, who lived in the United States. He confirmed it once when Mike Brown called him to the university office for an interview with Radio Switzerland.

The conversation had turned, in a civilized manner, to the financial crisis and American consumerism when Mike interrupted him:

"Well, listen, Ernesto, everyone knows that Americans are imperialists who don't have a hundred grams of brain matter in their heads. A nation of cavemen, incapable of culture, who believe all the lies their governments feed them. How can the world move forward like this, poisoned with Coca-Cola and french fries?"

It wasn't a rhetorical question. It had been a friendly question, perhaps even accommodating, for the interviewee.

Ernesto replied:

"Fortunately, there are you Europeans, who are very intelligent; and we Latin Americans, who are very wise and know how to distinguish truth from lies, good from evil. True, Americans have so little brain that when they crossed the Atlantic and stopped being Europeans, they had to start inventing new things to compensate for the sudden loss of intelligence, perhaps due to overly turbulent voyages. Not only have they been inventing strange things since the days of Benjamin Franklin and Thomas Edison, but even today they persist in shaping this horrible digital world full of computers, the internet, most of the innovations in *high tech*, and almost everything the world consumes at the start of this century, even if the final products say 'made in China.' They are so unintelligent, and we are so clever, that to hide this difference, they became a horrible empire that colonized, dominated, and exploited us. And since we are so wise and intelligent, we didn't want to be rude and let them do all that to us. That's why we've specialized in lamenting our bad luck, which is explained by the lack of intelligence of the Americans."

Mike Brown had to cut him off due to lack of time. The news was about to start at ten in the morning.

Saturday, July 11. Dow Jones: 8,146
Sacramento, California. 6:19 PM

They had sat at a table against the wall. María José said she was going to the bathroom to wash her hands, and Ernesto stayed behind, dipping tortilla chips in the spicy sauce. Almost every Saturday afternoon, they went to a *Chili's* or an *On the Border* because Tex-Mex food never let them down. While waiting for the chicken fajitas, Ernesto studied the tiles on the table, the huge inverted cauldron that served as a lamp, the paintings with Frida Kahlo and Diego Rivera-like delusions. A naive painting had caught his attention: a vast desert with cacti and a snake on a red dirt road.

"*Native*," he recalled. "In Old French, *naif* means native, from the Latin *nativus*."

At that moment, he received a text message from his brother. Their grandfather had died. Last Monday. Four days ago. Nacho hadn't wanted to tell him earlier because it was pointless; he knew Ernesto wouldn't make it in time. It would have only made things worse. Everything had happened very quickly. He asked Ernesto to please forgive and understand him.

Ernesto remembered that since the day before, he had been accumulating questions for the old man. He couldn't ask them all. The old man, the dear old man, was half-deaf, and phone communication was becoming increasingly difficult. They were questions to ask him one day when he returned, calmly, without rushing, questions that, for the life of him, he had never asked despite how important they were. Why did they never talk to me about Grandma Rosa? Why was Grandma Rosa taken to die in my room when her son, Cacho, was in town, that guy everyone loved and said was such a good man? Was he really that good then? Why did I and my siblings, who were so little, have to listen every night to the delusions of an old woman who was dying? *"Put out the fire, the fire there at the feet! My doll, where is my doll? My doll is going to burn alive, my doll!"* Grandma Rosa seemed so happy before she fell ill. She was always laughing, always with her garlic and onions and eggs freshly stolen from a red hen. And her verses by José Martí that she didn't know were by José

Martí. Why did you divorce Grandma if she was as good as you always said? I would have liked to ask her this same question, but she died before you. That's why I'm asking you. Why was it never known where my uncle Ismael went? I know he had been involved in the Tlatelolco uprising, I already know that. But why did he have to disappear? And why did everyone have to take his disappearance as something normal? Or it seemed normal because no one said anything about the long-haired uncle. Just a photo of him smiling with a thick mustache. That's why you can't imagine him screaming in pain. Only smiling. Of course, that's why I never asked. Who goes around asking about something normal? Why do I have so many questions about so many normal things and feel like they're now underground? Forever underground, you, Grandma, Uncle, my mother, my questions. A little bit of me. A little bit of me is underground and the rest is slowly drying up. Like a plant in the desert, the roots are the last to dry out.

The large two-handled inverted pot that served as a lamp floated above the table, and his questions barely clung to the edge. Grandma had one just like it, very similar. She made sweets in the patio every Saturday with the fruits I rescued from the pigs. Since they couldn't eat them, Grandma turned them into sweets. Why did she say Aunt Guadalupe was a whore? She had a child out of wedlock. But her man had acknowledged the child and took both of them to live on the other side. Who knows if they didn't pass through here. At least they left together. The three of them, wandering around, loving each other, arguing, fighting, separating, finding each other again without anyone giving them a familiar hand. So why did Grandma insist that Guadalupe was a whore? Maybe it was spite. That can be deduced. But why had she been in prison before leaving as an undocumented migrant? And why did Grandpa Rojas die alone, with no one going to the house where he was dying. Not even his children went. Why? Why the hell didn't it occur to me to ask them all that when I was still on the other side? Something so simple, so easy as a question. Surely it would have been enough to scratch a little and then other questions would sprout like clusters of grapes. Why, after Grandpa Rojas was buried by some neighbors, were there always flowers on his grave? They say that everyone, the children, the daughters-in-law, even Grandpa and Grandma Rosa, brought her flowers on Sundays. Why, if they had never gotten along? Why did you never tell me anything about this, Grandpa? Did I have to be the one to ask you?

At that moment, María José returned with a smile. She sat down. She looked around, looked at him, and then turned serious.

"In a bad mood again."

Sunday, July 12. Dow Jones: 8,146
Socorro, New Mexico. 1:25 AM

He wouldn't stop crying, and I had no choice but to give him one. I might have gone too far, I know. My wife always told me not to lose my patience, but after all, I'm only human. The thing is, that day I hadn't slept well, and at work, every day was worse, and there was always something missing on the table or too many bills to pay. Day and night, hearing that "beep-beep" from the barcode scanner.   Yogurt-paper-bread-hamburger-phone-card-Coca-Cola.

Have a nice day
You too.

And there's always some idiot complaining about something or looking at me sideways because I'm not going fast enough, or pretending not to understand me because of my accent. Who can put up with that?

And by the time I got home, María would leave because she also had to take care of her own. Poor Machito, he got hit a lot, one time after another, and if Guadalupe hadn't been deported, it wouldn't have happened. María says that Maicol turned out like that, half-blind and with attention problems at school, because of all the hits I gave him on the head. But that's not true. As kids, we all got a slap or two, and that didn't make us so distracted. The other day, the teacher came to me with the story that Machito doesn't pay attention in class. He can't add, she says, but I've seen him do subtraction: 10-5 = 5. María says it was a fluke, because Machito is a bit slow from all the hits I gave him as a kid. That's not true because we all got a few hits at some point, and we know how to subtract. Besides, who knows if he's even my son. I used to tell Guadalupe that, by my calculations, she must have slept with someone at the border. Those things women do to get some benefit, to make it easier. But she kept saying no, and I wanted to go on Don Francisco's show where they do the DNA test for free, and she kept saying no, that it wasn't necessary. Every time I brought it up, she'd go quiet. The worst part is that knowing how to add is more important than knowing how to subtract, María tells me, and I tell her that I don't even need to know how to add because all that mess is done by the barcode scanners. But I don't think the teacher has the right to scold Machito because the law reserves that right for parents. She's not going to tell me how to raise my son. And don't exaggerate either. I only hit Machito hard once, when he was about a year old and couldn't sleep and cried all night for Lupe. I gave him a punch, it's true, I admit it, his little nose bled, and instead of stopping, he cried more. So on top of the punch, I threw him against the wall.

That's how he stopped crying, and to this day, Machito is so well-behaved. Lupe would be proud of him, I tell him, but he doesn't seem to care.

Thursday, July 16. Dow Jones: 8,711
Terra Bella, California. 9:15 PM
Lupita picks up the handful of strawberries, but the strawberries slip from her hand again. Because of this clumsy hand, Lupita complains, her poor back can't take it anymore. The dirty, cracked hand barely moves, it hardly hurts. But her back and stomach do. Lupe tries to

pick up the strawberries again, but they seem to move away as if in a tunnel. In half an hour, her shift will end. It's eight hours of bending over the earth, under the sun that gives life to the strawberries.

But the half-hour stretches like the tunnel that keeps the five strawberries out of her reach.

They say that nowhere else do strawberries grow so big and red, though they don't know how they are over there, Lupita used to say. At Walmart, they smell better, José would say, because of the air conditioning. They're not strawberries, they're strawberry giants, clean and neatly arranged in transparent boxes.

Yesterday was the same. 110 degrees from noon until five in the afternoon. In the shade, Ramón says, 110 degrees in the shade. How much is that, José? Like 40 or 45 degrees over there. Then it dropped to 105, and they say that by the end of the shift, it was 95, and the sun was hitting from below. The good thing is that the sun moves and doesn't always burn you on the same side. Sometimes it's like it's hitting from below, Lupita would say. And when it hits from below, it's like falling into a dark tunnel, and the sun is the end.

José laughed. The things a young woman imagines. She had brightened up the work since she arrived two weeks ago. José always managed to work on a line nearby, and she felt safer when she saw him approaching with his hands that were like strawberry-picking machines. The picking machine, they called him. But when he passed near Lupita, it was as if he slowed down, like a swimmer decelerating to rest.

At one point, she lost sight of him. Lupita prayed to God that the last half hour would pass quickly, that the end would come, that José would say, "Finally, we're done for today," even though Lupe knew her basket hadn't filled up as fast as yesterday and that they were probably keeping an eye on her for low performance.

But the strawberries, as big as five beating hearts, kept tumbling down the temple stairs, and the sun didn't let up. Until her back gave out, and her face hit the dry earth, and a smell of blood and strawberries, thick as sea salt, erased the sun at the end of the tunnel. A warm river ran down her legs, watering the mother earth that at that hour was like a thirsty dragon. "Miguelito," was the last thing Lupe said, almost shouting, but unable to shout, said José.

Michael, said the picking machine who hasn't returned today, was the child the new girl carried in her womb. They say they're now looking for someone to give the compensation for the deceased girl.

Good Reader's Notes:

252 X

CRISIS